SANDS OF DESTINY

In Africa the Foreign Legion stands between the tribesmen with their dreams of the Great Jehad, and the traders and colonists of the peaceful settlements. Secret agent Lieutenant Crispin de Corville discovers a treacherous plot to unite the tribes and wrest arms from the Legion. Fighting his way across the desert, Corville, while in disguise, must learn the tribesmen's plans as he conveys two women to safety . . . realising that the sands of the desert are indeed the 'Sands of Destiny'.

Books by E. C. Tubb
in the Linford Mystery Library:

E. C. TUBB

SANDS OF DESTINY

Complete and Unabridged

LINFORD
Leicester

First published in Great Britain

First Linford Edition
published 2009

Copyright © 1955 by E. C. Tubb
All rights reserved

British Library CIP Data

Tubb, E. C.
  Sands of destiny - -(Linford mystery library)
  1. Secret service- -Africa- -Fiction.
  2. Peacekeeping forces- -Africa- -Fiction.
  3. Insurgency- -Prevention- -Fiction.
  4. Suspense fiction. 5. Large type books.
  I. Title II. Series
  823.9′14–dc22

  ISBN 978–1–84782–873–6

Published by
F. A. Thorpe (Publishing)
Anstey, Leicestershire

Set by Words & Graphics Ltd.
Anstey, Leicestershire
Printed and bound in Great Britain by
T. J. International Ltd., Padstow, Cornwall

This book is printed on acid-free paper

1

Sidi bel Abbes

Beneath the sweltering heat of an African sun the city of Sidi bel Abbes rested in uneasy peace. A strange blending of the ancient and modern with tall, glaring white concrete buildings shouldering low, dried mud and baked brick of native architecture, its winding streets filled with the sleek bodies of high-powered cars and the dull-eyed, patiently plodding camels of primitive transport. Here, in West Algeria, the East met the West and both suffered a little from the merging. Tourists, still in white from Northern suns, self-conscious in their tropical dress, cameras slung about their neck, wandered and stared at buildings that were old when their own countries were young. Around them clustered hordes of shrill-voiced beggars and vendors of cheap souvenirs, thrusting at each other and

1

filling the somnolent air with raucous sound. A Hadji, a stately Arab, cool in his loose white burnoose, his turban bearing the green thread of one who had made the pilgrimage to Mecca, walked slowly towards the mosque where the Muezzin, tiny as he stood at the top of the slender tower, raised his voice as he called the faithful to prayer.

'Allah il Akbar.'

A normal day in Sidi bel Abbes.

Crispin de Corville thought so and, as he stared at the well-remembered scene, he felt the tugging of a faint nostalgia. He had arrived here in 1930 — five years ago. A raw recruit for the Foreign Legion and, since then, life had demanded, and given, much. They had taken him, had the Legion, and from a soft, kind-hearted son of an English nobleman, had turned him into a tough, ruthless soldier of the most famous army in the world. Promotion had been swift, his gift for languages, his knowledge of French and Arabic, his previous training in the Officer Cadet Corps of a public school had soon lifted him from the ranks into the coveted officer status. Now, as he stood tall and slim in his uniform, his shoulders bearing the insignia of a lieutenant, he smiled a little as he remembered those first days when, still a civilian, he had arrived at the headquarters of the Legion.

Automatically he stiffened and returned the salute of two legionnaires, their faces brown and hard beneath their kepis. He looked after them for a moment, proud of their military bearing, then frowned as a native, a ragged, dirty, scavenger of the streets, glared at the broad backs of the two soldiers and spat after them.

For a moment he was tempted to avenge the insult then, as he remembered who and what he was, forced himself to dismiss the incident as of being no importance. There was always trouble between the natives and the Legion. Even the city Arabs hated the trim men in their blue and scarlet. In that they were no different from the war-like tribes of the interior, the Bedouins, the Touregs, the dozen lesser-known tribes of nomads who were forever plotting to overthrow the rule of the Ferangi and to establish their own despotism. Dangerous

3

these tribes were, a smouldering fire of incipient rebellion, all too ready to be whipped into flame by some fanatic preaching the necessity for a Jehad, a holy war which would stain the sands of the desert with innocent blood and ensure the faithful's path to Paradise over the broken bodies of the unbelievers.

Between those blood-hungry tribes and the overthrow of peaceful law and order were the iron men of the Foreign Legion.

Corville sighed as he thought of it, feeling the familiar sense of strain and anticipation which he had felt for too long now. Peace was something that had to be worked for and the slightest relaxation would release the ever-present threat of the Jehad. Adjusting his kepi the young officer strode down the narrow streets towards the bleak, dried mud barracks of the Legion Headquarters. A group of new recruits passed him as he walked, pale-faced men, poorly dressed with here and there someone who, once, had obviously been a gentleman. Watching them Corville thought of the hundred reasons a man might have for losing himself in the anonymity of the Legion. Heartbreak, financial failure, escape from responsibility, from crime even, for the Legion asked no questions and a man could lose even his name once in the uniform of the famous corps. He stepped aside as they swung into the barrack square, most of them carrying a small bundle over one shoulder, all of them staring interestedly at the place which was to be their new home. The sergeant in charge, a grizzled veteran of many battles, snapped his arm in salute as he passed the officer, his hoarse voice bawling sharp commands.

'Eyes right! Eyes front!'

Some of them didn't understand him. Most of them had yet to learn French but the commands were unmistakable in any language and they dutifully turned their heads in salute to the officer watching them. Corville stared after them as they passed within the barracks, there to be issued with uniform, allocated beds, instructed in the organisation of barrack-life and to be readied for the training that would start at dawn next day.

A training that they would never really finish for the full five-year term of their voluntary induction.

Next to the dried mud wall of the compound a bleak, white-walled building of concrete reared towards the cloudless sky, and to this building Corville walked. The soldier on guard snapped to attention, his Lebel almost springing to the salute. Corville returned it and, with a sigh of relief, passed into the shadowed coolness of the interior.

'Lieutenant de Corville,' he said to a soldier sitting behind a desk. 'I am expected.'

'Yes, sir. Colonel Le Farge has given orders.' The soldier pressed a button. 'A moment, sir. I will have someone conduct you to the Colonel.' He stared with undisguised interest at the young officer. 'May one ask the officer if the news is good?'

'One may,' said Corville drily, 'but one should not expect an answer.' He turned as a second soldier, this one in un-dress uniform, appeared from a door at the rear of the building. 'Lieutenant de Corville?'

'Here.'

'If you will come with me, sir? The Colonel will receive you immediately.'

Corville nodded and followed his guide.

Colonel Le Farge was a man who appeared to have been withered by the tropical sun. A small man, his face so lined and wizened as to give him almost the appearance of a monkey, his eyes bright flecks of gleaming intelligence peering from beneath thick, shaggy eyebrows which, like his hair, had long ago lost their original colour and were now as white as paper. He looked up from where be sat as Corville entered the room, and dismissed the escort with characteristic abruptness.

'Go.'

'Yes, sir.' The soldier withdrew and Le Farge glared at Corville.

'Well?'

'Not well,' said the young man deliberately. He had long since learned that the Colonel's manner was quite innocuous and refused to let it annoy him. 'I've just returned from . . . '

'I know that,' snapped Le Farge. 'I sent you. Well?'

'Rumours.' Corville shrugged. 'As usual the bazaars are full of them. None of much importance and none of them new.'

'Bazaar talk!' Le Farge sneered his contempt. 'Is that all you have to report? The lowest of my agents could have done as much, I expected better from you than that, Corville.'

'If you will let me finish?' The young man stared at the irate face of the Colonel. 'As I said the bazaars are full of the usual gossip. I'd expected that but I had to make sure.' He paused. 'I met a camel driver, one belonging to a train that had come from the region of Onassis, and he told me something very interesting. It would appear that a new voice has been raised in the tents of our brothers. A voice which cries to the faithful to rise and throw off the yoke of the Ferangi.' Corville stared at the intent face of Le Farge. 'Is this news to you?'

'No.'

'The camel driver mentioned a name, Hadji Hassan.'

'Meaningless.' Le Farge bit his lips with annoyance. 'With the organised pilgrimages any Moslem worth his salt would have gone to Mecca and thus acquired the title of 'Hadji'. Hassan could be an adopted name, the name of a benefactor, or a name taken for a purpose. There is no lead there.'

'Then why let it worry you, sir?' Corville dropped his bantering mood as he saw the seriousness on the face of the other. 'Some local zealot trying to whip up a holy war, the desert is full of them, but they all land up in much the same place. Prison, or, mostly, an unmarked grave. The tribes are too sensible to rise at the urgings of any one man. They have been chastened too often to believe that mere words and a belief in Allah can sweep aside the forts and silence the Lebels of the Legion.'

'You think that?' Le Farge shrugged. 'Listen. Corville, you have been in the Legion five years. Am I correct?'

'Yes, sir.'

'You came here from England, never mind why, though I know your history better than you know it yourself.' Le Farge smiled at the other's expression. 'It is essential to employ men we can trust in the Arab Division and, naturally, I had to check on you. Your father was an Englishman, a noble, and your mother was French. They parted, again never mind why, and your mother took you to live with her in France. You were educated in England and, a few years after leaving your public school, joined the Legion.' The old man leaned forward over his desk with a suddenness that surprised the young man. 'Why, Corville? Why did you join the Legion?'

Corville didn't answer. Le Farge was within his rights to enquire into the history of any man, within his rights too to confront that man with his knowledge as he was doing now, but he had no right at all to ask questions of such a personal nature.

'You do not choose to answer?' Le Farge shrugged, a typically Gallic gesture. 'Very well, I cannot make you answer, but equally so, you cannot prevent me from hazarding a guess. Your father, did he not vanish after your mother and he parted? Was there not some scandal? Never mind my young friend, though, if I were to be asked to give a reason for your being here, I think that I should be able to come very near the truth.'

'Would you?' said Corville stiffly. 'May I remind the Colonel that it is hardly his place to question me as to my private affairs.'

'You have no private affairs,' snapped the old man. 'You are a soldier, a servant of France, and everything you do must be done with that in mind.' He waved his hand at the young man's expression. 'Oh, I know. You have served your term and are free to resign your commission at any time you choose, but somehow, my friend, I do not think that you will.'

'The Colonel knows what he knows.'

'The Colonel knows a good man when he sees one.' Le Farge slumped in his chair and waved irritably at a droning fly. 'Sacre! What are we talking about? Have some wine and wash the taste of the desert from your mouth. It is not for us to quarrel, you and I. We are comrades of

11

the Legion and our enemies are around us, but not within.' He produced a bottle and filled two glasses with the thin, acrid wine of Algiers. 'A votre sante!'

'A votre sante!' Corville drained the glass and watched while the old Colonel refilled it. At times like this military protocol was relaxed though discipline was as rigid as ever.

'You know,' said the old man reflectively. 'Sometimes it seems strange to me to find how little people know about what we do. To the tourists the Arabs are a harmless part of the scenery. To the business people they are someone with whom to trade, bringing in their wool, skins, a little gold and dried dates to the market for sale for cloth, trinkets, and other goods. To the horse trader they are the breeders of the finest flesh on four legs, and to the Legion they are the Devil incarnate.' Le Farge rose and crossing the room rested his hand on a large-scale map of the area. 'Look at it. Desert, kilometre after kilometre of it, sand dotted with the scanty palms of oasis and encampment. Men live there, wild, savage, untamed men. Proud of their independence, direct descendants from the old slave traders who convoyed hundreds of groaning blacks to the slave ports on the coast. From these men sprang the corsairs and human wolves who ravaged the inland sea for hundreds of years. They are wild and untrammeled, uncivilised as we know civilisation, and like wolves they strain at the leash. One day they will break out and when they do . . . ' He made an expressive gesture.

'They will not break out,' said Corville positively. 'A few small, scattered out-breaks perhaps. A fort or two attacked, some men killed, a few others tortured, but that is all. The Legion will destroy a few villages, shoot a few men, imprison others, and the whole thing will blow over as it has always done.' He sipped at his wine. 'My Colonel is starting at shadows,' he said affectionately. 'He is beginning to dream of the great Jehad which will sweep the Ferengi into the sea.'

'You laugh?' Anger gleamed for a moment in the deep-set eyes of the old man. 'You mock?'

'No.'

'You jest then? That is good, but there is a time for jesting and a time to be serious.'

'I am serious,' said Corville. 'I remember Hollenfort and what we found there.' He shuddered. 'Those women used their knives well in that place. We had to shoot twenty men and it was an act of mercy for which they begged.'

'Yes,' said Le Farge sombrely. 'Native women have a skill with their knives. Once . . . ' He shuddered and gulped at his wine. 'Never mind now. It is over, but my brother? Shall I ever forget him?'

Corville sat while the old man stared blindly at the map before him, reliving again the memory of a sudden attack, the defeat of an isolated garrison, and the frenzied shrieking of tormented men as the native women tortured the captives with their razor-edged knives. After a while Le Farge drew a deep breath and, when he stared at the young officer, his face was bleak with a grim resolve.

'It is said, and said true, that the onlooker sees most of the game. Here in this office, like a spider in a web of intrigue, I gather the threads of a mat of knowledge which you, working as you are too close to the source, must fail to recognise.' The Colonel slumped in his chair and reached for the wine. ''Rumours', you say, and dismiss them with a shrug. 'A local fanatic', and again you ignore the obvious. I cannot afford to do that. I must take every single item of information into account and from it weld a united whole. If I fail to do this, then the dam will break and a tide of blood will stain the sand to a deeper red than it has ever known.'

'The Jehad,' whispered Corville, and stared with new respect at the old man. Le Farge nodded.

'The Jehad. Not a Jehad, you note, but *the* Jehad, the great holy war to smash the rule of France and set up the rule of native tribesmen.' He shrugged at Corville's expression. 'Never let yourself be deluded by appearances, my young friend. What, after all, is the Legion? A relative handful of hardened troops, trained, yes, and with an iron discipline which has made them the most famous corps in the world, but,' he leaned forward, 'they are still a handful. Should the Arabs arise at one time, should they simultaneously ride from the desert and attack the towns, and should they isolate our forts and cut our lines of communication, then the Legion would be swept away and blood would rule instead of law and order.'

'It could never happen,' said Corville positively.

'It has never happened,' corrected Le Farge. 'And why? Because the French Secret Service of which this, the Arab Division is part, has seen to it that all previous attempts to stir up a mass uprising have been doomed to failure. As an agent of the Arab Division you should know that. As an officer of the Legion you must know it.'

'I know it,' said Corville quietly.

'Then you know what is my task,' snapped the Colonel. He looked at the map again. 'For thirty years I have served the Legion and France. For thirty years I have baked in the sun and listened to intrigue and forestalled plot after plot. I recognise the signs now. I can tell, sense if you like, when the pot is coming to the boil again.' He snapped his hand hard against the top of the desk. 'A new voice preaches rebellion in the tents of Onassis. Nothing, you say, and you are right — if it were that alone. But add other factors. The theft of a shipment of rifles from a warehouse. A dhow found to be carrying large quantities of ammunition. A second, outward bound, and full of pearls and hashish. Add the fact that the bazaars are full of whispers and that no tourist is safe in the town after dark. Add murder of a prominent liberal Arab who preached cooperation with the French and remember the fire at Sali Bearena, a fire in which the records of many notorious agitators were destroyed. Take the mysterious disappearance of a man from a foreign power, a man who was reputed to be able to speak Arabic like a native.' Le Farge stared at the young officer. 'Well?'

'Pearls and hashish to buy guns and ammunition. The records destroyed so that the agitators would not be molested by the police. Stolen rifles, an Arab tribesman would do anything for such a rifle, and the fanatics preaching in every tent and encampment.' Corville nodded. 'It begins to make sense.'

'It makes very good sense,' said Le Farge grimly. 'As I said, the pot is reaching the boil again. We must take it off before someone gets burned.'

'You have a plan?'

'Yes.' Le Farge emptied the bottle of wine into his glass and sipped at the thin, red fluid. 'Before the tribes can stage a successful revolt they need arms. Some have been smuggled through past our watch on the coast, but as the smugglers ask a high price for such weapons, and as the tribes rarely have wealth in other forms than camels, goats, horses and rugs, they will not be able to buy many of them. The Sheiks, of course, already own modern rifles, but that cannot be helped.'

'How about rifles captured during previous outbreaks?'

'Rifles need ammunition,' reminded Le Farge. 'The nomads are extremely waste-ful in their use of cartridges, they have to be, every young man must learn to shoot and that takes ammunition. So, even though they may have rifles already, and certainly there are a great number of Lebels hidden in the tents, yet they still need ammunition for them. The obvious place to get it is . . . ' He looked questioningly at Corville.

'A garrison,' said the young man. 'Or a fort, or even, though I doubt if they would attack it, the arsenal at Marojia.'

'Exactly. So, in order to squash this incipient hell, we must know just where to expect the preliminary attack. If we can crush that, beat them back and punish them for breaking the peace, then we may, and I repeat, may, be able to avoid bloodshed.' He stared at the young man. 'That is your job.'

'Mine?'

'Yes. You have been among the Arabs before and can speak like one. You know their ways and could pass where another man would be discovered and tortured to death. You are to mingle with the camel drivers, they always seem to know what is going on, and from there ferret out the

19

truth.' Le Farge sighed. 'I may be starting at shadows, I hope to God I am, but if there is anything in what I feel, then we must take every precaution.'

'You wish me to stay in the city and to report to you personally?'

'No. You are attached to the garrison at Onassis and you must return there. Make your way in disguise and, when you discover anything of value, report to Colonel Marignay. He will forward the information to me in cipher.' He stared at the young man. 'Any questions?'

'Am I at liberty to time my own movements or must I report within a certain time?'

'Use your own discretion. I shall inform Colonel Marignay to expect you. Once you have reported to the garrison you will resume your normal command.' Le Farge hesitated. 'Be careful. I have reason to believe that information as to the Arab Division has been reaching ears for which it was not intended. Two agents have mysteriously vanished and one other was found yesterday, horribly mutilated and still alive.' Le Farge swallowed. 'He died in hospital a few hours after he was found.'

'I understand, sir.'

'I hope that you do.' The old man dropped his hand familiarly on the other's shoulder. 'Find out what you can and report it to the Colonel. Take no risks other than those you cannot avoid.' His grip tightened a moment. 'I am depending on you, my young friend. See to it that you do not let me down.'

'You may trust me, my Colonel,' said Corville quietly. For a moment the two men stared at each other, one so old, the other so young. Then Corville snapped his arm into the salute, turned, and without a backward glance marched from the office.

Behind him Le Farge sighed, stared at the map a moment, then reached for a new bottle of wine.

2

Death in the Desert

Heat. A simmering bowl of the brightest azure for a sky in which the lambent ball of the sun glowed like the feral eye of some angry god. From it, reflected from the undulating dunes of the desert, torrid heat blazed with furnace-like fury, sucking the moisture from man and beast and turning the fine sand of the desert into an impalpable dust that rose in soft, cloud-like plumes from beneath the plodding feet of the camel train.

A big train it was, fully two score of heavily laden beasts together with outriders mounted on sleek Arabian horses whose manes were decked with brilliant scraps of cloth and whose bridles and saddles were studded with silver. Grim men these outriders, hawk-faced, their eyes ever watchful as they scanned the desert for signs of a raiding party, many of them with their long Jezails, old-fashioned muzzle-loaders chased and ornamented with silver, resting across their saddle bows. Others carried more modern weapons, Lebels and Mausers, with here and there a Schnider. Swords too, they carried, the heavy-bladed scimitars and in the belts of all were slender bladed knives.

Corville rode on the neck of a haughty camel, his face half-hidden in a fold of his burnoose, and let his eyes drift over the surrounding terrain. For three days now he had worked as a camel driver and during that time the caravan had pushed on with a speed almost unknown for desert travel. Sidi bel Abbes had long since fallen beneath the horizon and, to his surprise, instead of the caravan heading directly towards Onassis by the shortest route, they had made a swinging detour to the East. Now, riding as if part of his beast, the young officer let his mind toy with the problem of why an apparently innocent camel train should have both veered from its regular path, and be pushing on with incredible speed.

He thought that the answer lay hidden in the thickly wrapped bundles carried by more than half the camels.

How they had passed the inspectors at the town Corville didn't know. He had joined the train just before it had left the encampment outside of the city and, because they had needed an extra driver, he had been engaged with only token questions. The armed outriders had joined them on the second day and, watching them, Corville began to have an idea of what was behind the detour and the speed.

Guns.

Smuggled weapons for some rebellious tribe loaded and passed by bribed inspectors now on their way to delivery at a rendezvous deep in the desert away from the prying eyes of the Legion. Rifles from Italy, Greece, the Turkish States and perhaps from foreign countries further north. Weapons to arm the tribesmen so that they could rise and turn against their protectors and lawmakers. Guns to blast innocent traders and settlers, villagers and peaceful natives, Legionnaires and tourists. Guns to set the desert aflame.

And there was nothing the young officer could do about it.

Sitting on the camel as he steered it across the featureless sands he had evolved and discarded a dozen schemes to destroy the lethal load. All of them were impracticable. If he was discovered tampering with the loads he would die, not quickly, but with all the diabolical ingenuity of the East. Being buried alive with only his head protruding above the sand for the vultures to peck out his eyes would be nothing compared to what the outriders would do to him. They would strip him naked and then, even if they did not discover he was a Ferengi, they would tie him to a horse and drag his body over the desert until the skin had been worn from his bones. Or they might choose the fire-torture, or that inflicted by the thin, razor-edged knives and which turned a man into ghastly abomination to whom death was a welcome relief. Corville shuddered as he thought about it and, beneath the loose burnoose, his hand touched the butt of his automatic as if to reassure himself that, should all else fail, he could still die a clean death.

The shouting of his fellow drivers attracted his attention and he stared ahead to where the foremost outriders had wheeled their mounts with a flurry of sand from beneath their hoofs and were now racing back towards the caravan.

'Toureg! Toureg!'

The word was enough. At the mention of the dreaded raiders of the desert, the so-called 'Veiled ones', or the 'Scourge of God', something like panic disorganised the camel caravan. For a moment men shouted and prayed to Allah then, with the fatalism of their race, settled down to fight or die.

Long-muzzled Jezails were loaded from powder horns and heavy bullets rammed home. Scimitars glinted in the brilliant sunlight and others, too poor to own sword or gun, whetted their knives as they prayed for compassion. Finally, after a brief flurry of activity, the caravan was ready to fight or die though, knowing the reputation of the notorious Touregs, Corville had little doubt as to the outcome.

Dust rose from the horizon, a swelling cloud of disturbed particles lifting and rising towards the harsh clearness of the sky. Figures became visible, the mounted warriors of the Toureg, their faces veiled against the sand and their bodies appeared to be one. Sound came before them, thin shouts and the deeper, more menacing sound of shots.

'Allah preserve us this day,' muttered a man standing next to Corville. 'Look at them! What chance does a humble driver of camels have against the Scourge of God?'

'Allah is wise,' said the young officer enigmatically. 'What is to be, will be. Peace, brother, maybe we die this day, but what is written is written and no man can escape his destiny.'

'So be it,' replied the man, and began to pray with hopeful fervour. 'Allah the all-wise, the all-compassionate, the all-knowing . . . '

Incredibly it seemed as if his prayers were answered. Directly towards the waiting camel train the Touregs rode. Directly towards the grimly waiting outriders and the trembling drivers, their mounts spurning the sand, their weapons glinting in their hands their veiled faces making them seem like beings from another world. Abruptly they reined. Sand plumed towards the mounted horsemen, hiding them, almost covering them with its fine grit, then it settled and, in solid array, the Touregs rested on their motionless steeds.

'Allah be praised,' shouted the man next to Corville. 'He has heard and answered my prayers!'

'Silence, dog!' One of the Touregs, tall in his saddle, stepped his horse forward and spat the words as if they hurt his mouth. 'Where is the leader of this caravan?'

'Here, lord!' A fat merchant, who, up till now had ridden in a covered palaquin, stepped forward, his thin beard almost touching the desert as he bowed, his fat hands washing themselves in invisible soap and water. 'It is I whom you wish to see, mighty Sheik. I . . . '

'You have too much tongue,' interrupted the Toureg. 'Have you that which we seek?'

'Aye, lord.'

'It is well.' The Toureg gestured with the short whip he carried in his hand. 'Proceed. By nightfall you should be at the oasis of Haroom. Camp there and, in the morning, we shall conduct our business. Follow!'

As he finished speaking he turned his horse's head and, without a backward glance, rode on into the desert, his men falling in line behind him. Immediately the air resounded with the shrill orders from the merchant, the camel drivers goaded their ungainly steeds into motion, and, before the Touregs had reached the horizon, the camel caravan was plodding at increased speed after them,

Corville was thoughtful as the day dragged on. The Touregs had acted totally out of character in not attacking the caravan. The fat merchant had expected attack, else why the heavily armed escort? But he had also seemed to be expecting the visitors. Corville shrugged, making a note to keep alert that night, and, reaching for his goat skin of water, allowed a little to trickle into his mouth.

He would have preferred wine, or, as no Moslem was supposed to touch wine or strong waters, cooled sherbert, but to a thirsty man water, even tepid and stale, is the most welcome drink of all.

Night fell before they reached the oasis. The sun sank with the abrupt suddenness of the tropic regions, the clear azure of the sky changed to a bowl of blackness glittering with stars, almost as if some careless jeweller had tossed a double handful of diamonds against the soft black velvet of space. Low on the horizon a swollen moon floated like a full-sailed ship over the gleaming sands and silence, the incredible silence of the desert, folded the caravan as if in a world of its own.

Corville was nodding with fatigue when they arrived. He jerked awake to shouted commands and slipped stiff-legged from his mount. First came the necessity of feeding and unloading the camel, watering it at the muddy pool which supported scant life for a dozen palm trees and a scattering of sparse vegetation. His duties over, he joined the rest of the camel drivers around a small fire and dipped his hands into the communal dish of cous-cous and boiled and spiced mutton. Dried dates followed the meal and long, cooling drinks of sherbert, an unaccustomed luxury for the humble drivers. Lying on his side Corville listened to the idle gossip of the chattering men.

'By Allah I swear it,' said one, and the young officer recognised the man who had stood beside him while waiting for the Tauregs. 'Even as I waited for the angel to sweep down to carry me to Paradise my prayers were answered and the Scourge of Allah halted in their tracks.' He gulped at the sickly sweet sherbert. 'This tastes the pleasanter because of it. Never did I think to drink again.'

'If your throat had been cut from ear to ear, still would you drink,' laughed a man, a squat, scarred-faced man whose dingy turban showed the green thread of a Hadji. 'But this I will say, our leader, may dogs defile his grave, has never thought to give such as we sherbert before. Rather rotten meat and sour water, not couscous and sherbert. Allah must have moved his bowels for compassion for him to do this thing.'

'So you say!' Corville set down his untouched bowl of sherbert. 'I am new among you,' he explained. 'I know not the ways of your master. Is this indeed a rare treat he has given us?'

'Rare?' The Hadji spat into the sand. 'I have slaved for the spawn of Shaitan for twenty moons now and this is the first time he has cast more than a curse my way. And yet,' he added reflectively, 'he did push us hard.'

'Hard? My bones are sore from the jolting and my tongue is as the leather of the harness.' A third man, old and wizened, dipped his bowl into the urn and slobbered as he gulped the sherbert. 'He must hate his camels to treat them so. More, two days more, of such speed and bones will litter the sand. Not even the Ferengi would treat men so.'

'The Ferengi!' The Hadji spat. 'Infidel dogs!'

'They are as Allah made them,' said Corville, and tipped the contents of his bowl into the sand at his side. 'Who are we to question the workings of Allah?'

'Allah is all-wise,' agreed the Hadji impatiently, 'But Allah has infinite patience and we have not. How long must we tolerate the infidel? How long must we listen to their jeers? It is said that three Ferengi spat on the Muezzin at the Mosque of El Farid. Is that a good thing?'

'It is a bad thing,' said Corville, who knew the tale to be a lie. 'If it be true then Allah should smite the unbelievers with his sword of fire.'

'If it be true?' The Hadji glared at the young man. 'If? Doubt you my word?'

'Not so.' Corville bowed his head in submission. 'And yet a man may hear a tale from one man, who heard it from another, who heard it from yet a third. Could Shaitan have started stories to arouse unrest?'

'Allah defend us from Shaitan,' droned the man who had prayed. He seemed to be half-asleep and, as he lifted his bowl to his mouth, spilled the contents over his filthy burnoose.

'Allah defends those who defend themselves,' said the Hadji seriously. He yawned. 'Allah, but I feel tired. May the spirits of air and water watch over us this night. May . . . ' He yawned again then, falling as a tree falls, toppled almost directly into the fire. Corville saved him, pushing the recumbent form away from the flames with the sole of his shoe, his nostrils wrinkling to the smell of the singed hair of the other's beard. He glanced around the fire.

All the drivers seemed either asleep or about to fall asleep. Corville nodded as he saw it, his suspicions confirmed then, to allay any watchers, he deliberately filled his bowl from the urn and, turning his head, pretended to gulp his fill of the sherbert. Carefully he tipped the contents onto the sand, yawned, stretched, yawned again, then fell flat on his back, his head turned away from the fire so as to avoid the betraying reflection of firelight from his eyes. Lying there, every sense alert, he strained his ears and listened.

Time passed, how long he did not know, but he forced himself to lie quietly despite the fact that several ants had found their way inside his burnoose and had sunk their mandibles into his flesh. Finally, just as he was about to rid himself of his tormentors, he heard the scuff, scuff of slippers and the sound of voices.

'Are they asleep?'

'Yes, my lord,' whined the voice of the fat merchant. 'I gave them sherbert well tainted with a certain drug which will make them as dead until tomorrow's dawn.'

'It is well,' said the voice of the Toureg leader. 'And yet it would be better should they not live to see another dawn. Dead tongues cannot wag, merchant. I would rest more easily should these dogs greet the new sun with sightless eyes.'

'That cannot be,' said the merchant hastily, then resumed his whine. 'Think you, lord. The Ferengi know when I left the city of Sidi bel Abbes. They know the duration of the journey to Onassis whither I am bound. Should I arrive so late as to arouse question, or arrive without the drivers I have employed, then eyes will be sharpened and much harm will be done to my trade.'

'Your trade.' Contempt thickened the

Sheik's voice. 'What is your trade to me, dog?'

'Less than the sand beneath the hoofs of your steeds, Sheik El Morini,' snarled the merchant. 'And yet it is a strange thing that it was to me that you came for aid. I . . . '

'Mock me not you dog!' Corville tensed to the hiss of indrawn breath. 'See this steel, of Damascus inlaid with writings from the Koran which gives the metal great power against devils and succubi. I doubt me not that it would sink readily into your heart. Shall I test the potency of the blade?'

'Nay, Lord,' stammered the merchant. 'I did but jest.'

'Jest? Then you would not deny me a smile at the sight of your blood?'

'I have eaten your salt,' babbled the fat merchant, now in a terror. 'I have shared your bread. You cannot kill me now.'

'You are safe beneath the laws of hospitality until the next dawn,' admitted the Sheik. 'Yet do not trifle with me man of too great flesh. It comes to me that you and those like you are the first to sell their dignity for Ferengi gold. It would be as well for you to remember that. Remember too that the Veiled Ones have a long arm and that their power does not end with the ending of the desert.'

'Why speak to me so,' whined the merchant. 'Have I not done as I promised? Here I have brought you many rifles from distant lands. Good weapons with which to slay the infidel. I . . . '

'Are the guns the same as used by the Ferengi?'

'The Foreign Legion? Lebels? Yes, it was as you so ordered.' The whine increased. 'Other weapons would have come cheaper, lord, but these rifles are scarce and difficult to obtain. Much gold I had to spend in having them shipped across the water. More to close the right eyes and seal the right mouths. Of profit I do not speak, it is sufficient that I serve you, but the risk! Aye the risk!'

'It would be a greater risk should you fail to serve,' said the Toureg coldly. 'Much have we of the desert stood from you and yours. Now, either you are with us or against us, there can be no middle path.' A slippered foot came into Corville's range of vision. 'Are you certain that these dogs are as dead?'

'Certain, mighty Sheik.'

'So?' There was the subtle scrape of steel sliding from leather. 'It may be that they lie with ears open to our words. Test them.'

'Test them? How?'

'Fool! Can a man resist the thrust of a knife?' The Toureg stooped and deliberately thrust the point of his dagger into a man's arm. 'So, this one at least sleeps well. The others . . . '

'Wait, lord!' The fat merchant stepped before the tall nomad. 'Think of what you do. These dogs have no idea as to what we carry and why we are here. Leave them in peace I pray you for the love of Allah. Take the things I have brought, give me the gold you have promised, and let me be on my way. With the rugs you have carried here to exchange for the loads they will not suspect that anything has occurred between us. A little hashish perhaps,' the merchant's shrug showed how tolerated the drug traffic was by the natives, 'but that is all. It will seem as though you desired sport with us and there will be no loose tongues to set the Ferengi on their guard.'

'The Ferengi! The unbelieving dogs! The infidel, the hated of Allah and the loved of Shaitan! Death to the Ferengi!'

'Aye, lord, but softly. Time to talk of death when we have driven them to the sea. In the meantime, let us act with caution and tread the path of true wisdom. Is it not written that what will be will be?'

'It is so written,' agreed the Sheik, 'but it is also written that what a man is then so also is what he will become. And there are other writings in the sacred books of Allah. Yet what is your fear to me?'

'Think, lord, and you will see the hidden wisdom. Guns have I fetched you, many guns, and there can be more, many more if . . . ' He paused, suggestively, and Corville could almost see the man's instinctive gesturing with his thumb and forefinger.

'Gold,' said the Sheik. 'You know that we have little gold.'

'And yet you could obtain more? Not gold, but other things? Money, the paper used by the Ferengi is of value, gems and precious stones, small things that a man could hide and spend for guns in the markets of the world. Money, Sheik?'

'I have no money.'

'A goat can be milked more than once,' said the merchant suggestively. 'If so then you will need me and what I can offer. Find gold, my lord, and I will find rifles,'

'I can also find rifles,' said the Sheik grimly. 'One does not need gold to obtain Ferengi guns. They are waiting for us to take, bullets too, plenty of both.'

'The forts?' The merchant's voice revealed his doubt. 'That's madness. To strike now would be to warn the Ferengi and . . .'

'Strike?' The Toureg stepped closer, his slippers throwing sand into Corville's face. 'What mean you? Speak.'

'I have heard the rumours,' babbled the merchant. 'In the bazaars they talk of it, in the coffee houses and in the places where dancing girls move to the delight of men. The Jehad.' The oily voice dropped a little and became sly. 'Tell me, lord, is it not so?'

'You know too much,' whispered the Sheik. He stepped even closer,

'I know what I know, lord.' The merchant chuckled. 'The Ferengi are worried, that I know, and many soldiers are to be seen in the streets of Sidi bel Abbes. There is talk of strengthening the forts and men are always ready to leave on forced marches. Even the Spahis . . . ' He choked, gurgled, tried to speak and then, with a horrible sound toppled and fell heavily to the sand. He fell within inches of Corville.

'Fool,' gritted the Sheik. 'Die for the dog you are.' He turned as a man stepped quietly towards him. 'Well?'

'The camels are unloaded,' said the man respectfully, touching his breast, lips and forehead in salutation. 'The guns are as we expected.' He glanced casually towards the dead merchant. 'Your orders?'

'Send a rider to the tribe and warn them to prepare for the attack. Slay these fools,' he gestured contemptuously at the sleeping drivers. 'The rest, recruit or kill, they are good warriors and will serve to stop a Ferengi bullet.'

'As you wish, my lord. Onassis?'

'Aye. My spies have told me that they have a new commander there now. Colonel Marignay, a man new to the desert and our ways.' The Toureg laughed with a peculiar soundlessness. 'He is a man of strange methods. Once a month he assembles all his men into the compound, drills them, addresses them, tires them out for his personal glory. Even the guard in the watchtower is so drilled.' He laughed again. 'Thank Allah that the sun has turned his reason for the benefit of the true believer. Fort Onassis will provide us with many guns.' His voice faded as he walked away, and Corville shivered to the sweat of sudden urgency.

He had to get to Onassis to warn Marignay before the Touregs could attack.

Of the dead merchant he gave not a moment's thought. The man had deserved to die. Anyone did who sold guns for gold, arming the very men who would kill those to whom the merchant and those like him would appeal for protection. Coupled with his direct violation of the law he had drugged the drivers, and, for all Corville knew, the outriders too. They were safe, as the Sheik had so cynically said any man was good enough to stop a bullet and they would probably agree to join in the attack both from hope of loot and love of fighting. The camel drivers, those poverty stricken unfortunates, without tribe, or pride, or possessions, they were to be sacrificed beneath a butcher's knife to ensure their silence.

And unless Corville moved fast he would be among them.

Carefully he wriggled away from the sleeping men, thankful that the Sheik had not chosen him for the 'test', knowing how difficult it was for any alert men to prevent an instinctive flinching from a painful wound. Behind him, a little to one side, a horse snickered as it stamped restlessly and a man, a dark shadow in his loose burnoose, the long barrel of his Jezail sticking past one shoulder, looked in guarded watchfulness at the restless beast.

Corville thinned his lips as he made his

slow and careful way towards the guard. He might be alone, he could have a companion, or there could, as there sometimes was, three or four men watching the valuable horses. Corville was lucky, the man was alone.

He collapsed as the officer hit him on the base of the neck, sagging towards the sand, his figure suddenly limp and lifeless. Rapidly the young officer donned his burnoose and slung the Jezail over his shoulder. Cautiously he approached the horses and had almost reached them when a man hailed him from the darkness.

'Hamid? What do you here?'

Corville didn't dare reply. Even though he could speak Arabic like a native yet he knew that he could not hope to assume a voice he had never heard. Instead he stooped, appeared to examine the sand at his feet, then gestured towards the unseen guard.

'Hamid. Are you ill? What ails you?'

As he spoke the guard moved out into the moonlight. Corville gestured again and, as the man came within reach, struck heavily towards the jaw. He missed, the man swaying aside and, before the young officer could silence him, had shouted a warning into the night.

'Sacre!' The automatic was in Corville's hand and his finger pressing the trigger before the echoes could die away. Again the pistol blasted fire, this time towards a third guard and, as the man toppled screaming to the sand, Corville drew his sword and slashed the reins of the tethered horses. Within seconds they were free, he had mounted one, and was shrieking and yelling at the top of his voice, striking at them with the flat of the sword and lunging his own mount hard against them.

They broke and ran from the screaming demon who had aroused them from sleep, their hooves making a dull thunder as they raced across the desert and with them, riding low over the cruppers, Corville rode like a man possessed.

He had gained a little time, but only a little. The horses would soon be recaptured, Toureg horses were too well trained to bolt and not return, but he had shaken off immediate pursuit. Now, without water, without a saddle, with only the stars to guide him and limited ammunition between him and death at the hands of any small raiding party he might contact, he rode into the silence of the night.

To warn Fort Onassis.

3

Sergeant John Smith

Sergeant John Smith rose in his stirrups and stared with narrowed eyes across the burning sands before him. A big man he was, tall, sitting his mount with easy grace and trained skill. His eyes were grey, his skin burned to a copper brown and on his left cheek, the writhing scar of an old wound traced its furrowed path from the corner of his eye down past the corner of his mouth. The puckering of the scar had lifted the upper lip a trifle so that, at all times, he seemed to be perpetually sneering at a life that, for him, had proved no bed of roses.

Behind him, marching in close file over the dunes, a small patrol of legionnaires moved with mechanical precision, the long barrels of their Lebels glinting in the sun, their blue and scarlet which, together with their white kepis, comprised their uniform, making an unnatural splotch of colour against the eternal brown sand of the desert. They were dressed in full marching order with water canteens, blankets, field packs, ammunition and bayonets. Looking at them the sergeant felt quiet pride at the military bearing of his men and gestured them to continue marching while he scanned the sands ahead. His corporal, a stunted veteran of many wars, halted at his side.

'Any signs yet, John?' He spoke with the easy familiarity of an old friend and the sergeant answered in the same way.

'None. The caravan should have arrived a day ago and here we are, two days march from the fort, and still no sign of it.'

'Raiders?' Corporal Lambert spat with thoughtful accuracy at an unwary scorpion. 'The Toureg are restless again I hear, and with them are some Bedouin and Riff tribesmen. A rich caravan would be tempting bait to such as they.'

'Perhaps.' The sergeant's cultured tones were in startling contrast to the rough, untutored speech of the corporal. 'And yet we should have heard had they been attacked. A survivor, maybe more, for the tribes rarely exterminate all, especially after they have won the battle.' His voice hardened. 'It is only the weak and the helpless who meet the fate of their women's knives. Wounded legionnaires and harmless traders.'

'Should we continue the march then, John?' Lambert stared after the departing column. 'Our water is low, another two days and we shall all be thirsty, and the nearest oasis is at Onassis.'

'We will continue the march,' ordered the sergeant. 'I am swinging the line around so as to head back tomorrow.' He pursed his lips. 'It is as the Colonel ordered. All legionnaires to be assembled in the compound at dawn three days from now.'

'He is a strange one, that Colonel Marignay,' said Lambert. 'The men hate him for his harshness and murmur over their wine. It is not good for men to feel so.'

'I have heard nothing you have said,' snapped John Smith. 'I am a sergeant and, if I thought that the men were restless, I should have to report it to the officers. I do not like to see good men punished for speaking their minds. You comprehend?'

'As my sergeant orders,' said Lambert. 'I am a man of discretion, no?'

'No.' The Sergeant twitched the reins of his mount. 'Hold onto my stirrup, lazy one, and run beside me to the head of the column. I will ride ahead, to the summit of that high dune and there see what I shall see.' The mount reared a little as he touched its sides with his spurs, then settled down to a loping canter. Lambert ran beside it, hanging onto the stirrup leather, and released his hold as they drew abreast of the head of the marching column. The sergeant spurred his mount again after the corporal had left him and, slipping and sliding on the loose surface, guided his horse to the summit of the high dune.

There he halted, a picturesque figure against the skyline and, shading his eyes, stared out over the desert that stretched before him like a frozen sea.

He frowned, stared, then, taking a pair of binoculars from a case slung around his neck, lifted them to his eyes.

'Lambert.'

At the cry the corporal left the head of the column and ran towards the mounted officer. 'Yes, sergeant?'

'Look!' John pointed towards a tiny spot close to the distant horizon. 'Here.' He handed the corporal the field glasses. 'Tell me what you see.'

'A man,' said Lambert after a moment. 'An Arab. Toureg I think, and from the way the vultures circle around his head I doubt me that he has long to live.'

'I will go to him,' decided John, then looked down as Lambert held the reins. 'What is it?'

'It could be a trap,' reminded the dour corporal. 'It would not be the first time that an apparently wounded man has killed his would be rescuer. That man is a Toureg, and you know the Touregs, he will kill you even if it takes his last breath to do so.'

'He is sick, probably dying, I cannot watch him die without aid.'

'The dunes could be full of mounted warriors waiting to attack you.' Lambert clung more firmly to the reins. 'Wait at least until the men can march with you.'

'So you think it could be an ambush?' John nodded as he thought about it. Lambert was right. Using a decoy was a favourite trick of the warring tribesmen and, as the corporal had warned, the dunes could be full of armed men ready to shoot and kill both for the sake of the weapons he carried and because he was one of the hated legionnaires. The sergeant hesitated, staring at his men. They would fight any odds, fight until their last bullet had been used and they fell back on the long, sword-like bayonets slung at their sides. But they were but few and the Touregs many. Should it be a trap then he would be responsible for their deaths and worse for the loss of their arms to the hordes ever-ready to threaten the peace of the desert. And yet, despite that knowledge, he saw a man in pain and knew that he had to help him.

'Deploy,' he ordered. 'Watch. I will ride forth to that man. If, as you suspect, it is a trap, then I alone shall die. If not, then we may learn of the caravan we seek.'

'But, John . . . '

'Enough! It is an order.' Without a backward glance, the sergeant spurred his horse and rode towards the tiny figure ahead. Lambert stared after him, his eyes thoughtful, then snapped quick orders to his men.

Automatically they obeyed, un-slinging their rifles, checking the loading of the weapons then, with rifles at the ready, loped at increased speed towards the diminishing figure of their sergeant. Lambert grinned. He had obeyed his orders; but should trouble arise, the men would be ready to go through hell itself in defence of their beloved sergeant.

John knew nothing of his corporal's preparations. He rode, his eyes watchful, towards the tiny figure ahead and as he came nearer, he saw that the man staggered and fell, rose to stagger a few more paces only to fall again. John had seen men act so before. Men who were at the last stages of exhaustion from heat and thirst, literally dying on their feet with only their indomitable wills enabling them to keep going. Once they lost that will they would collapse, would lie on the sand to let the sun suck the last moisture from their bodies, unable even to beat off the hungry birds who would swoop down to peck the eyes from their still-living prey.

The sergeant did not alter his pace, ten years in the Legion had made him wise to the subtlety of the Arabs and, even though the distress of the man ahead could be genuine, yet it was still possible that the Toureg had deliberately caused that condition in one of their prisoners so as to deceive suspicious eyes. Finally, still watching the desert around, he came up to the man and stared down into a face tormented with pain and thirst. A face he recognised.

'Lieutenant de Corville. Crispin!' The sergeant flung himself from his horse, snatched his canteen, and, half-supporting the near-dead man, poured a trickle of tepid water between the blackened lips. Corville shuddered, opened his eyes and tried to snatch the precious container of water. The sergeant restrained him, knowing that too much water could kill as surely as too little, knowing too that Corville, in his state of mind, was hardly responsible for his actions. Gently the scarred sergeant moistened the parched lips, allowed a small amount of the clear fluid to enter the mouth, gently massaged the swollen throat until Corville had managed to swallow it then, the initial stages over, gave the officer a half litre of water to gulp down with animal-like savagery.

'More.' Corville held out the empty cup. 'Water. I beg of you give me water.'

'Later.' Smith screwed the cup back onto the canteen and slung the container over his shoulder. 'Later, sir, you can have as much water to drink as you wish. Not now. Now it would bloat your stomach, give you great pain, could even do what the sun and the sand have failed to do. It could cause your death.'

'Yes,' said Corville, and blinked as he stared at the scarred face above his own. 'I know you, do I not?'

'Sergeant Smith, sir, of the garrison at Fort Onassis.' John smiled. 'You should know me, sir. I am of your command.'

'Onassis!' Corville forced himself to his feet. 'Sergeant! The fort is about to be attacked by a party of raiding Touregs. It is imperative that the Colonel be warned of the danger. I . . . '

Corville sagged, his body suddenly falling limp and helpless to the sand. Heat and exhaustion had finally weakened him and the knowledge that now, after all this time, he could relax with the comforting knowledge that his message was in safe hands. He muttered as the sergeant picked him up and set him across the saddle of the horse, living again in his dream world the nightmare ride over the moonlight desert with his enemies snarling at his heels as they tried, mad with rage, to stop the one man who could betray their plans. They had been clever had those Touregs. They had mounted the camels, stripped of their loads for added speed, and had guarded the nearest routes to Fort Onassis. Corville had almost died when he rode into that trap and had barely escaped with a wounded horse, leaving three dead men behind him.

Then had come bitter days of searing heat and frigid nights of shivering cold. Thirst had come, and hunger, but of those two thirst was by far the worse. The horse had collapsed and he had been forced to shoot it to put it out of its misery. How long he had wandered with only the stars and the sun to guide him he never knew, but somehow, it may have been the sight of a familiar face or the familiar uniform, he knew that he was yet in time and that now he was safe. So he slumbered the deep, uneasy sleep of exhaustion while the sergeant, supporting the limp figure on his saddle, walked his horse back to his waiting men.

'Toureg?' Lambert stepped forward as the sergeant drew near. 'Riff? Bedouin?'

'Neither.' John didn't want too many of his men to learn that their officer had been found in Arab disguise. He called the corporal to one side. 'It is Lieutenant de Corville. He warned me that the Touregs were about to attack Onassis and asked me to warn the Colonel.' He glanced at his men. 'We must return to the fort at once. Inform the men that this is a friendly Arab we have found, the less who know of the lieutenant's services among the Arabs the better. You understand?'

'Perfectly.' Lambert hesitated. 'The lieutenant, is he well?'

'Exhaustion. I have given him water and will later give him more. He will recover soon, we caught him just in time, but another few hours would have seen the birds at his eyes and not all the water in the oceans could have saved him.'

'It is well,' said the corporal seriously. 'The lieutenant is a good man.' He looked at the sergeant. 'Your orders?'

'We return to the Fort. Open order with arms at the ready. Post flankers and vanguard. The lieutenant will ride my horse and I will remain at his side. Quickly now! Action!'

It was smoothly done. Men detached themselves from the column to form the vanguard, marching several hundred metres in advance of the main body. Others took up similar positions to either side, watching the desert around for danger and keeping their fingers on the triggers of their Lebels. Lambert watched the men take position then, his voice carrying to the furthest man, snapped the order to march. In a compact unit, ready for any form of trouble, the legionnaires with the unconscious officer slumped across the horse and their sergeant at his side, marched back towards the fort that was their home.

The attack came at dawn on the second day. It started with the spiteful crack of a rifle and a man, one of the legionnaires on guard, screamed as he fell, clutching at his stomach, and vomiting blood. A second rifle fired, a third and then the brightening day was rendered hideous with the yelling cry which all the legionnaires had learned to hate and fear.

'*Allah il Allah! Mohammed il akbar!*'

They came like a rush of white-cowled ghosts, seeming to rise from the very sand, their rifles spitting fire and lead at the little band of legionnaires. Corville had woken with the sound of the first shot. He had almost recovered, from his journey and, though still thin and gaunt from privation, was well on the road to full recovery. Now he forced himself from automatically taking command and snapped quick instructions at the sergeant.

'Take command, Smith. I do not want the men, and more especially the Arabs, to know that I am a legionnaire in disguise. Once they learn that then my usefulness will be over.' He smiled at the scarred face of the sergeant. 'Anyway, you are as capable of taking over as I. Do so.'

'Yes, my lieutenant.' Smith turned and shouted quick instructions but, even as he gave his commands, the men had anticipated them with the cunning of years of experience in desert warfare.

The first charge of the yelling Touregs was met with a hail of lead and white-burnoosed figures tumbled to the sand and there stained it with their ebbing blood. Again the savage raiders flung themselves against the beleagured men and again the long-barrelled Lebels sent them to an early Paradise. But it seemed that mere death alone could not stop the savage charge for, to men who firmly believed that Paradise waited for any man who died while attacking the

60

infidel, death was nothing, an open door from the harshness of desert life to the promised land flowing with milk and honey, with pleasant gardens and eternal youth and fresh young Houris to serve their every whim.

And so they charged again and again, yelling their faith that there was no God but Allah and that Mohammed was his Prophet. And each time they charged there were fewer Lebels to answer their screaming defiance.

Men died in the sand as they blasted at the burnoosed shapes. Men of many nations and many languages, united beneath the common banner of the Legion and proud to die among the men with which they had lived. Lambert, his eyes glinting over the barrel of his rifle, swore a medley of oaths as he pumped lead towards the attacking Touregs.

'Les Cochon! Chein! Sacre Bleu! Pigs! Swine! Devils! Take that you son of a fatherless mother! And that, you spawn of hell. And that from Francios who you killed at Hollendoft, and for Pierre who you staked out for the ants to eat two years ago.' With each imprecation he fired at the Touregs and more than one of his skilfully aimed bullets met their targets.

But the death was not all on one side.

Legionnaires died too, not so fast, nor as many, for they had burrowed into the sand so that only the slender barrels of their rifles and the tops of their kepis showed above the desert. But they died from sheer weight of numbers for a man can only shoot at one target at a time and when he is faced with five targets, all shooting, all advancing, all screaming to Allah and eager to die, then it takes more than a Lebel to save him.

And so they died, their blue and scarlet daubed with the bright hue of blood, as they lay gasping in the sand. Some died cleanly, shot between the eyes or in the heart. Others were not so lucky.

Crouching beside the motionless body of the horse, one of the first to die, Corville worked the bolt of a rifle with practiced ease and sent lead whining across the sand towards the advancing figures before him. Again he fired, again and again until the barrel grew too hot to touch and until his groping fingers found empty leather where bullets should have been. Smith crawled towards him, his scarred face a mask of blood and sweat, a flesh wound in his upper arm staining his once-trim uniform with blood.

'Things are bad, my lieutenant. It seems that these devils will not withdraw until we are all dead.'

'It is I they are after,' said Corville grimly and fired at a burnoosed shape ahead. 'You remember the message?'

'Yes, sir. But what can messages avail now?' Smith ducked as lead thudded into the saddle an inch from his head. 'We are very near the fort, I cannot understand why they should attack us when so near.' Again he ducked and Corville grunted as something like a hot iron traced a path across his forehead. He swore as he wiped blood from his eyes, then smiled at the anxious face of the sergeant. 'A flesh wound, it is nothing.'

He stiffened as he caught a vestige of sound above the firing, and stared hopefully at the sergeant.

'Did you hear that?'

'Hear what, sir?'

'That. Listen.' The firing lulled and faded away almost as if each man was straining his ears to the vagrant sound.

It came again, louder, clearer, thin and distant but unmistakable.

The notes of a bugle.

Hearing it the legionnaires raised a cheer then, as if afraid of losing their vengeance, began firing with a total disregard for their expenditure of ammunition, blasting at the Touregs as if their Lebels were machine guns, spraying the desert with leaden death and sending more than one shapeless figure to his desired Paradise.

For a moment the Touregs hesitated, seemed about to charge again, then, as the bugle sounded nearer and louder, broke and ran across the undulating dunes towards their hidden horses.

Within seconds, it seemed, the desert was devoid of all life but for the fleeing shapes of horsemen, the huddled bodies of the dead, and the grim-faced, wounded, cursing remnant of the column of legionnaires.

'Eh bien,' said Lambert joining Corville and the sergeant. 'It was warm while it lasted, no?'

'Too warm,' said Smith drily. 'Me, I can do without such heat.'

'I managed to avenge Francios, my brother,' said Lambert. 'I swore that five should die for what they did to him at Hollendoft. Pierre also, I have yet to kill three for him, but there will be another time, yes?'

'Yes.' The sergeant stared towards the horizon to where the ranked kepis of a marching column had appeared in view. 'Just in time,' he muttered in English. 'Another few minutes and . . . ' He broke off, staring at the young officer, then shrugged and holstered his pistol.

Corville managed to stay out of the way while greetings were being exchanged and the legionnaire dead stripped of weapons and buried. The wounded were supported on crude stretchers for transportation back to the fort and the Arab dead were left where they had fallen. Perhaps their comrades would return for them or perhaps they would lie until sun and weather had turned them into bleached bones.

Either way it didn't matter and as the reformed column swung into the march back to the fort and safety, Corville felt a sudden elation. He had accomplished his mission and, with his warning, Colonel Marignay should be able to beat off the attack and, perhaps, crush the threatened rebellion.

He hoped.

4

Onassis

Fort Onassis was a squat, sombre edifice of sun-baked brick. It dominated a rocky pass, one of the main caravan routes to the East, and from its high, slender watchtower floated the tricolour of France. From its walls guards stared down at the surrounding terrain and, in the watchtower itself, the solitary figure of a watcher could be seen as he scanned the desert with field-glasses. A bugle sounded as the column came into sight and, by the time they had reached the thick walls, the guard had been alerted and the doors opened to admit the weary men.

Hostile eyes stared at Corville, still in his Toureg costume, and angry oaths reached his ears as men inspected the wounds of their comrades or looked for friends now lying in shallow graves. Hate ran high in Fort Onassis, hate of the savage raiders forever threatening their peace, hate of the sun, the restricted life, the insects, the heat, the monotony of the desert and, to this hate, was coupled a hatred of their commanding officer.

Corville saw the reason for that hatred as he crossed the pounded dirt of the compound towards his own quarters. A man, a legionnaire, stood in the burning sun, naked to the waist, his hands lashed to a cross-beam above his head, his back scarred with angry weals. He had been whipped and, as he stared at the red cross-cuts marring the brown skin, Corville felt a rush of anger towards the commander of the garrison. Men were punished in the Legion, and discipline was hard, but men were not, nor should they be, whipped. There were cells, dark and noisome holes, damp and alive with vermin. There were forced marches with full pack and little water. There were labour details and, in the most severe cases, the penal settlement in which men worked at road building as they served their sentences. But whipping was not allowed by the military code. To whip a man both degraded him and his companions and, listening to the idle mutters and watching the eyes of the legionnaires, Corville resolved to do something about it.

In his room, the door shut and locked, alone with the sergeant from whom he had no secrets, the young officer stripped, washed from a basin of tepid water, dressed in his uniform and, once again a legionnaire in every sense of the word, straightened with a new dignity.

'Why was that man whipped?'

Sergeant Smith shrugged and felt the bandage around the flesh wound in his arm. Like Corville, he had first received medical attention; the young officer had a strip of adhesive bandage over the wound on his forehead.

'I asked a question,' snapped Corville. 'Who ordered the whipping?'

'Colonel Marignay, sir.'

'Why?'

'It was said that the man cheated at cards. There was a row in the sleeping quarters. I investigated and . . . '

'Is it not usual for the men themselves

to attend to such matters?'

'Yes, sir.'

'Then why the exception?'

The sergeant hesitated. Corville knew that Smith, like all sergeants in the French army, had greater power and responsibility than is to be found in almost any other army in the world. In effect Smith had the authority of a second lieutenant in the British Army, and he could have issued his own punishment within limited degrees.

'Why was the man whipped?' repeated Corville impatiently. 'Come. Give me the reason.'

'I enquired whether the man would accept my punishment,' said Smith slowly. 'He agreed and I sentenced him to clean out the barrack room for a month and to lose half his wine ration for a week.'

Corville nodded. It was a light enough sentence and one that the man would have been grateful to accept.

'Well?'

'The Colonel learned what had happened and saw fit to override my authority. He ordered the man whipped. The first man he ordered to do the whipping is in the cells. He refused. The second is in hospital. He accepted.'

'What happened?'

'He had an accident,' said the sergeant deliberately. 'An unfortunate fall down the inner staircase. His nose was broken, his jaw, other injuries not so serious.' The ghost of a smile trembled at the corner of the sergeant's lips. 'For some odd reason he seemed to believe that someone, he didn't know who, attacked him.'

'I see.' Corville knew better than to question too closely.

The legionnaires had an incredible sense of comradeship and would have been certain to have avenged their disgraced comrade. The first man, the one in the cells, was probably feted with smuggled rations for his defiance of the unloved colonel. The young officer stared at the sergeant.

'Have you reported to the colonel yet?'

'Not yet, sir. It is not my place to supersede you. As my superior officer you will, of course, deliver your message yourself.'

'But you have alerted the guards?'

'Yes, sir. But I cannot do more without direct orders from the colonel.'

'Naturally.' Corville stared at the scarred face of the sergeant. 'Tell me, Smith, why haven't you tried for promotion? With your experience you would be certain to reach officer status.'

'Thank you, sir. You are good to think so.'

'I know so, man.' Corville frowned. 'Smith? That is an English name. Are you English?'

'Yes, sir.'

'I thought so. Why don't you want promotion?'

'There are two reasons, sir,' said the sergeant, stiffly. 'One, to achieve entry to the military school for officer examination I must take French nationality and swear the oath of loyalty. I was born an Englishman and, strange as it may seem to you, I prefer to die one.'

'But that can't be the whole reason?' Corville shook his head. 'I too am English but naturally I took the oath the same as we all do. At the expiration of my term, or if I resign, I can always resume my original nationality.' He looked at the sergeant. 'You said that there were two reasons?'

'The other is personal, sir.' The sergeant stepped towards the door, unlocked it, and held it open. 'Shall I conduct you to the Colonel, sir?'

It was polite, but it was definite and, as he followed the man towards the Colonel's quarters, Corville had to admit that Smith had been in the right and he himself in the wrong. Mentally he cursed himself for a fool for trying to probe. Before Smith could be accepted as an officer he would have to disclose his true identity for security checking. Obviously he didn't want to do that. The very name he had chosen to be known by, 'Smith', was proof of that.

Corville was still mentally kicking himself for his blunder when they arrived at the quarters of Colonel Marignay.

The Colonel was one of a dying breed. Brave, but without imagination. Stubborn, and yet who firmly believed that his stubbornness was evidence of a strong will. Ignorant, and relying heavily on his inferiors for his information and advice, both of which he disregarded whenever they came into conflict with his own ideas. No longer young he still retained the straight back, the trim figure and the thick hair of a man twenty years his junior. Now his hair was white, his hands thin and veined, his eyes not what they used to be.

He should have been retired years ago. Instead of that he had used his influence to gain the command of an isolated fort deep in the desert. There, so his superiors thought, he could do no harm and, like an old warhorse set out to graze, they had allowed him to spend his final years surrounded by the military discipline that he had known all his life. Corville had heard of him but as yet they had never met. The young officer's duties had kept him much in the desert where, in disguise, he had ferreted out information for Colonel Le Farge whom he regarded as the real commanding officer. For the purposes of the records, rank, and, more important, of allaying suspicion, Corville was attached to the garrison at Onassis.

The Colonel looked up from his desk as the young man entered, watched critically while he saluted, then gestured towards a chair.

'Sit down, de Corville. I hear that you had a spot of bother on your way here.'

'Yes, sir.'

'Twenty men dead.' Marignay shook his head. 'Bad, de Corville. Too bad. How did you come to let so many die?'

It was typical of the man that he should use Corville's full title. As typical as that he should automatically blame the young man for the dead legionnaires without first finding out the facts. Corville cleared his throat and stared at the Colonel.

'I have important information, sir, which must be sent at once to Colonel Le Farge at Sidi bel Abbes.' He frowned at the expression on the old man's face. 'I understand that you were informed of my coming, sir?'

'No.'

'Has no messenger reached you?'

'None.'

'I see.' Corville frowned down at his

hands, his mind busy with thoughts. Le Farge must have sent the message and, if it hadn't arrived, then it must have been intercepted on the way. It was a grim reminder of the incipient rebellion. Normally traders were allowed to pass unmolested. It was only the rich, unarmed caravans that tempted the raiding tribes.

He stared at the old man.

'I have gained information that a massed raid is due to take place against Fort Onassis shortly. I understand that it is your habit to assemble the men in the compound at regular intervals. The Arabs know this and they plan to attack at the next such assembly.'

'Tomorrow?' Marignay blinked. 'Impossible.'

'Why is it impossible, sir?'

'The tribes are at peace with us. Why, only a short while ago I was entertained by one of the desert Sheiks. Sheik El Morini, a Toureg, an educated man who assured me that he only desired peace so that his tribe could tend their herds unmolested.'

76

'Did you believe him?'

'Of course.' Marignay smirked. 'He gave me a gift, a damascened dagger, the hilt set with jewels and the blade inscribed with writings from the Koran. It is a work of great antiquity and I shall treasure it after I have retired to my Villa in the south of France as a memento of my stay here.'

'You are unwise to accept gifts of such a nature,' said Corville quietly. 'I know well the dagger you describe. I saw its twin at the oasis of Haroon when it was used to murder a scheming merchant. I travelled with the caravan that carried guns for your 'peace-loving Sheik' and I heard him plan to attack Onassis at your next assembly.' He leaned forward in his eagerness. 'I tell you, sir, that the fort is about to be attacked. The battle out on the desert where twenty men lost their lives was wholly to prevent me reaching here with the news.'

'Ridiculous!'

'It is not ridiculous, sir.' Rapidly Corville told the Colonel what he had learned, how he had escaped, and how he was rescued. 'So you see, sir, it is imperative that the men remain alert. A full assembly with full dress uniform would give the Touregs the opportunity they need for a surprise attack. Fort Onassis is surrounded with hills, each giving plenty of cover for waiting attackers. Once they reach the walls of the fort we shall have almost insurmountable difficulty in driving them back. The whole thing is the essence of stupidity.'

He regretted those words the moment he had said them. Right or wrong Marignay would now hold his precious assembly even if only to prove to the young officer that he was not stupid. He would continue on his own way because to do otherwise would be to admit that perhaps the young man was right and he was wrong. Marignay could never do that.

'Ridiculous,' he repeated. 'There isn't the slightest essence of danger. You are imagining things.'

'Did I imagine twenty men dead out in the desert,' snapped Corville. 'Was that proof of the peaceful intentions of Sheik El Morini?'

'We have no proof that it was he who instigated the attack. It could have been anyone, or, more than likely, a wandering band of nomads hoping to get some rifles and ammunition.'

'Nomads would not dare to attack an armed column of the Legion,' said Corville. 'And you know it, sir.' He sighed as he saw the stubborn set of the other's mouth. He knew that Marignay hadn't been long enough in the desert to learn of the subtle ways of the Arabs. He had served most of his time in France and probably thought of the Legion as a glorified police force. To him it was incredible that anyone should dream of attacking a garrison. Marignay had heard of such things happening but, despite that knowledge, he simply couldn't believe that it would ever happen to him.

Corville wished that the old commander, Colonel Frenshi, had managed to survive his last bout of fever. If he had Corville would have been free of his worry. Frenshi wouldn't have stopped to argue or assert his superiority. He would have manned the walls, loaded his guns and waited, snarling like a trapped tiger, ready for anything the desert could bring.

But Frenshi was dead.

'I think that you are worrying yourself unduly, de Corville,' said Marignay drily. 'I can assure you that there will be no attack on this or any other garrison.'

'I wish that I could share your optimism, sir.' Corville tried not to be sarcastic. 'But may I enquire why you saw fit to punish one of the men in the way you did?'

'I whipped him, or rather, I had him whipped.' Marignay made a negligent gesture. 'The alternative was to put him in the cells and we have too many men in the cells as it is.'

'It was an unorthodox punishment, sir,' reminded the young officer. 'The man would be within his rights at making a complaint.'

'He may if he wishes.' Marignay sounded as though the subject was totally unimportant. 'I shall consider whether to forward such a complaint if it is ever made.'

'It won't be made,' promised Corville.

'You know that none of the men would ever do that. Is that what you relied on when you ordered the whipping?'

'You are insolent, sir!'

'I am truthful, sir. I do not care to see the men on whom I rely treated like dogs.'

'Be careful, sir,' stormed Marignay. 'Do not think that, because you are an officer, you are immune from punishment. I could have you cashiered for insubordination.'

'You could try,' snapped Corville, now almost shaking with temper. 'But I am not one of the men who cannot defend themselves against a petty tyrant. I shall appeal to Sidi bel Abbes and inform them of your conduct here, I would go so far as to say that it is leading directly to mutiny. Commanders like you, Colonel, have a nasty habit of dying during the very first engagement. Usually from a bullet in the back.'

'How dare you talk to me in that manner!' Marignay surged upright from his desk and stood, his face red with anger, staring at the young man. Looking at him Corville knew that he had gone too far. As a soldier it was his duty to obey, not to taunt his superior officer no matter how incompetent he might be. He could complain, yes, but in disobeying the Colonel he was guilty of mutiny and for that crime there was no excuse. He swallowed his anger and tried to calm the old man.

'My apologies, sir,' he stammered. 'I did not mean to threaten, only to warn. It is not wise to treat men with contempt. They will undergo the severest punishments without complaint, but no man who is a man can tolerate being treated as a dog.'

'The man stole from his fellows,' snapped Marignay.

'That is a bad crime,' admitted the young man, 'but even his fellows do not like to see him punished as you have treated him.'

'What else could I do?' Marignay shrugged. 'The cells are full as it is. The man stole, cheated, and the men themselves would have beaten him. I did it for them and, at sundown, the prisoner will be cut down, revived, and set about his duties. The incident will be over and forgotten.'

Corville doubted that. Some things are never forgotten, especially by a man who bore the scars of a whip on his back. Such things lead to mutiny or, as was most often the case, to desertion. In either event Corville could feel nothing but pity for the poor fools who tried either path. Mutiny never succeeded. The ringleaders were shot and the followers sent to spend their lives in a penal settlement. Desertion was even worse. Not from the Legion point of view, but from the man trying to run from his responsibilities. Few ever managed to escape at all. For those who did the desert itself must almost certainly kill them for, without food, water and transportation they were sure to die. Even if they escaped nature, it was a different matter to escape the human wolves who prowled the sands.

A lone legionnaire was a find indeed and many a poor devil had shrieked his life away beneath the daggers or in the fires of the permanent encampments at the big oases. Some managed to reach the coast after selling rifle and ammunition, clothes and equipment to the rare, friendly natives or sympathetic tribesmen they met. A few others adopted Islam and became Moslem and so rid themselves of the dread taint of 'unbelievers', but not one in a hundred ever managed to desert with success.

And yet men still tried and, while they were treated as Marignay had treated the thief, they would always try. Corville made a mental resolve to report the colonel's conduct to headquarters as soon as possible. Marignay was both dangerous to himself and to the Legion, and the quicker he was retired the better.

But first he had to make his peace with the colonel.

'I was hasty,' he admitted. 'I should not have spoken as I did. But I have been travelling in the sun, almost died from exhaustion, and the battle wounded me.' He touched the strip of plaster on his brow. 'Such things leave a man not himself.'

'Of course.' Marignay was suddenly affable again. 'You will join me in wine?'

Without waiting for an answer he produced bottle and glasses. 'Here, try this. I had it brought me from the vineyards of France. None of this thin, arid Algerian wine for me. No. I like the best and this . . . ' He sipped and smiled. 'Perfect.'

It was good wine, even Corville had to admit that, and he felt his tension slipping away as he sipped the ruby liquid. Here, sitting in the fort, surrounded by thick walls and armed men, he felt safe for the first time since he had left Sidi bel Abbes. It seemed incredible that tribesmen could ever storm the walls and beat down the defence and yet, remembering Fort Hollendoft and other forts which had fallen to the attackers, Corville felt a sudden chill so that he shivered a little. Marignay noticed it.

'You feel cold? Fever perhaps?'

'No. Just someone walking over my grave.' Corville smiled as he saw the colonel frown. 'An English saying, almost impossible to translate.' He held out his glass for more wine. 'As you say this is excellent wine. Burgundy, of course, vintage?'

'1897.' Marignay let a little of the wine roll around his tongue before swallowing it. 'A famous year for Burgundy. 1903 was perhaps, just as good, but wine, like music, improves with the keeping.' To Corville's surprise the colonel winked. 'I have been saving it for a special occasion. Tonight, at dinner, you will see what I mean.'

'You intrigue me.' Corville relaxed, feeling the reaction from too hard endeavour seeping through his bones. 'About the message I must get to Colonel Le Farge. Have you decided as to how best to get it to him?'

'Tomorrow,' said Marignay with a casual wave of his hand. 'We will discuss it tomorrow.'

'Tomorrow will be too late,' reminded Corville grimly. 'You forget, the attack is due then.'

'Nonsense, my dear young fellow.' The wine seemed to be making Marignay almost overpoweringly affable. 'Sheik El Morini is coming to dine tomorrow evening. How can he do that if we are under attack?'

'The Sheik probably jests.' Corville was reminded of the Toureg's grim sense of humour when he had threatened the merchant. 'He will probably dine here but as the victor, not as a guest.'

'You annoy me,' said Marignay pointedly. 'Please to remember that I am your commanding officer. To doubt my word is tantamount to insult.'

'I apologise. No insult was intended.'

'I'm sure of it. You have perhaps had a touch too much of the sun? A passing weakness I am sure, but the entertainment tonight should quickly restore you to full health.' Marignay seemed secretly amused.

'You intrigue me.' Corville set down his empty glass. 'About that message . . . '

'Tomorrow.' Marignay paused with the bottle in his hand. 'Please do not mention it again'

'No, sir.'

'That is better.' The colonel poured the wine. 'You are young, de Corville, and have much to learn. There is a certain way to do these things, a time for work and a time for the social graces. You are an aristocrat, one of the old stock, and I am pleased to have you here as one of my officers. Captain Gerald, while a good soldier, yet lacks that little something which can turn even the desert into a garden.' The colonel set down the bottle and stared at the young man. 'Life is hard here, de Corville, and a man can be excused a touch of beauty. Because we live like animals is no reason to act like them.'

'No, sir.' Corville was a little puzzled at what the other meant. He arrived at the conclusion that the colonel had been drinking too much wine.

'We have guests,' said Marignay. 'Three of them.' He smiled. 'A man and two women, old friends who, when they found that I was to be in command here, asked whether or not they could come and spend a while at a genuine Legion fortress. Naturally, I agreed. You will meet them at dinner this evening.'

Women! In a desert fort which was due to be attacked at any moment! Corville wondered whether or not he was dreaming.

5

Invitation to Danger

There were, as Marignay had said, three visitors to Fort Onassis. Two of them, the man and the younger of the two women, were Americans. Dick Mason was young enough to still be swayed by the thought of adventure and old enough to realise that most of it consisted of dirt and poverty, discomfort and disease. His sister, Clarice, was fresh from her education and was rounding it off with a trip to the capital cities of the world. Both were rich, not obtrusively so, but with the easy grace of those without snobbery and yet without fear of poverty. The elder of the two women, a Miss Carson, had been engaged as travelling companion and secretary to Clarice and it was she who, on the basis of a slight friendship with Marignay, had persuaded him to invite the party to the fort. They had arrived by camel train two weeks ago and already desert life was beginning to pall.

It was night when they sat down to dine. A cool and rare breeze had sprung up from the hills, so cool that men shivered at their posts and thought enviously of their warm blankets in the stuffy barrack room. The night was clear with the dying moon setting towards the low horizon and, from time to time, the eerie cry of a jackal broke the deathly stillness of the tropic night.

Marignay had, despite Corville's opposition, invited the full officer strength of the garrison to dine with him. Captain Gerald, a dour soldier of the old school who remembered the days when the French Colonial soldiers grew handlebar moustaches in obedience to the tenet 'Plus qu'll est long, plus est ma force,' or 'The longer the whiskers the stronger the man,' sat grim and unsmiling at the right of the elderly Englishwoman. Colonel Marignay himself sat at her other side between her and Clarice. Corville sat between the young American and her brother and tried not to think of what would happen to her should the Touregs succeed in their attack. Inevitably the talk turned to the eternal subject of the desert.

'It's so mysterious,' sighed Miss Carson who, from casual reference, Corville knew to be named Susan. 'Looking at the bleak, eternal sands, one wonders what strange things it could tell if it could only speak. Brave Sheiks, mounted on gallant steeds, thundering through the night to the rescue of some princess carried away by rough tribesmen from the interior.'

'The only Sheiks I have ever seen,' said Gerald brutally, 'are fat, dirty, lazy men who leave all the work to their wives and think more of a goat than any princess ever born.' He gulped at his wine, making no secret of the fact that he found it more to his liking than the thin, raw, stuff that was the ration issue. 'Good wine this. Colonel. One day I too will be able to fill my stomach with wine fit to drink instead of the swill we get from the commissariat.' He glowered into his glass. 'One day I think I will take a bayonet and pay a visit to those who grow fat at the expense of the legionnaires.'

'The Captain has a grievance against the world,' explained Marignay to his guests. 'Himself a robber, he thinks that everyone is trying to rob him. A pity that he sees fit to forget that he is supposed to be a gentleman.'

'Gentleman? Pah! Call me a man and leave out the 'gentle'. One cannot be gentle in the Legion. One must be of iron, hard, cold, ruthless. One must kill or be killed.'

He reached for the wine. 'But nevertheless, I can still enjoy good wine.' He stared at the guests. 'Come, drink up, tomorrow you may not have a throat to drink with.'

'Gerald!' Marignay rose and glared at the captain. 'You may leave us.'

'Leave you?' Gerald staggered to his feet and deliberately winked at the elderly woman. 'I'll leave you fast enough. But I'll take the bottle with me.' He grabbed it, lurched, and half staggered through the door. Marignay looked apologetically at his visitors.

'A thousand pardons for what you have

just seen, but what would you do?' He spread his hands. 'The Legion breeds hard men and one must make do with what one has. It was not so in the Blues, then we had officers who were gentlemen. I remember one evening when . . . '

Corville sat and let the colonel's voice drift over the surface of his mind. He alone knew that Gerald was far from being drunk. The Captain had sensed the incipient terror and had arranged to leave the dinner table early so as to keep an eye on the defences. It had proved impossible to absent himself and so, with direct simplicity, the captain had managed to get himself thrown out. Corville wished that he could do the same.

He became aware of someone speaking to him and turned to face the young American girl.

'I beg your pardon,' he stammered. 'What did you say?'

'I asked you how long had you been in the Legion,' said Clarice. Her voice was low and her French excellent. 'Did I ask something I shouldn't?'

'No. Five years.'

'Do you like it?'

'Pardon?' Corville blinked and forced himself to pay attention. 'Sorry. I was thinking of something else.'

'I asked you if you liked it.'

'Yes, yes I suppose I do but . . . '

'But?'

'But sometimes I wish that I were home again. There is something about the desert, something almost alien, if you know what I mean. It belongs to a different time, a different race. We come here and yet, try as we may, we can never be a real part of it.' He warmed to the subject as he put his thoughts into words. 'Watch an Arab as he walks along the street. See his movements, and then stare into his eyes when he talks with you. You never really know him. His very thoughts are different than our own, his sense of values, his god even, though, I will admit, that Islam seems to be as good a religion as Christianity for some things.' He smiled at her expression. 'It's true, you know. No Moslem will touch alcohol in any form. He will obey the laws of hospitality and respect the rights and privileges of others of the same faith. Sometimes I've thought that it would be a good idea for all legionnaires to turn to Islam. That way we might be able to restrain the tribes a little better than what we do. At least it would save . . . ' He stopped, remembering the company, and to cover his confusion drank some wine.

'How interesting,' said Clarice. 'You were saying?'

'Nothing of importance.' He could not tell her of the torture that awaited infidels when captured by the raiders. 'Do you intend to remain long in Algeria?'

'Not long. Dick had some business to attend to and Susan got us this invitation to stay at a real fort.' She sounded like an excited little girl as she spoke. 'I've always wanted to see just what the Legion is really like and now I know. Gee, who'd have thought that I'd ever be able to say I stayed in a real fortress in the desert.' In her excitement she had slipped into English, much to the apparent relief of Miss Carson and, seeing that she was more at home in her own language, Marignay gallantly forced himself to speak it.

'You have been to my home, yes? A Villa near Toulon. I wait for the day when I can leave this sand and dirt and spend the few years I have left in idleness and memories.' He leaned a little closer to the elderly spinster. 'It is strange is it not, that we, who knew each other so long ago, should again meet as we did? Fate, the natives would call it, and, for once, I will admit that they are right.'

'It is strange,' agreed Miss Carson. 'I've often thought of the Legion and the men who live and die to keep the desert safe for travellers. Tell me, Colonel. Do you have many battles?'

'No. Some skirmishes perhaps, but nothing serious.'

Marignay laughed. 'Why, are you afraid of being carried off to ransom by some Sheik?'

'Do they do that? Carry people off to ransom, I mean?'

Clarice spoke the question to the company but her eyes never left the young face of the officer at her side. Corville nodded.

'It sometimes happens. The Riff tribes

are notorious for it, they used to be slavers in the old days, you know, and habit dies hard. They will capture a likely prospect, demand as much ransom as they think they can get, and then send the prisoner home again when it has been paid. They are quite ethical about it really. They will celebrate the payment with a great feast to which the prisoner is invited and they part on the best of terms.' Corville smiled. 'You see, to them it is merely a matter of business. Either side is aware of the ethics of the thing and neither will feel hurt or injured in any way. Sometimes the would-be kidnappers are caught and sent to a penal colony. They either escape or die. No native can work for long as a white man can. Their spirit breaks, or their heart, or they just will themselves to die. That is why they will fight so hard to avoid capture.'

'What if the captive doesn't pay his ransom?' Dick looked at the young officer and spoke for the first time. His voice was deep, pleasant, and Corville warmed to him as he spoke.

'Then it is not so pleasant. An ear

might be removed and sent as a reminder, a second ear or, perhaps, a hand follows. Then, finally, the entire head is usually delivered. If the prisoner's family are at all fond of him they have usually paid by that time and so it is rare for any captive to die.'

'And suppose a woman was to be captured?' Clarice looked eagerly at the officer. 'Would they do the same?'

'No. Women are of little value in the desert. Unless she were a rich man's favourite wife, a Sheik's daughter, or a person wealthy in her own right, they would not bother with her. If they did, and could get no ransom, then she would be sold to the highest bidder.' Corville smiled at the shocked expression on Miss Carson's face. 'The desert isn't the romantic place most people think it is. The tribesmen are still pretty medieval in outlook and slavery is still practiced deep in the interior. To the average Arab a woman is merely a chattel, as much a possession as his rugs, his tents, his horses and goats, and of far less value than either of those.'

'I can't believe it,' snapped Susan. 'Do you mean to say that you tolerate such conditions?'

'What else can we do?' asked Marignay. 'The desert is huge, we are small, and who can watch the comings and goings of every caravan.' He nodded as he poured more wine. 'We are not blind, we of the Legion, and we know that many a slave has been sold on the block, many a load of hashish has passed across the borders into Egypt there to be sold for guns. Pearls too have found their way into the markets of the world without anyone paying custom duty on them. But these are little things. We of the Legion must keep the peace and that is what we do.'

'You make the desert sound so unromantic,' complained Clarice. 'Sheiks who are fat, dirty men, and camels loaded with smuggled guns instead of rare spices. You've destroyed one of my favourite illusions.'

'Not all Sheiks are fat or dirty,' smiled Marignay. 'Tomorrow night you will see the Sheik El Morini who, I am sure, will be able to restore your illusions. He is tall and proud and a pure son of the desert. I respect him as a gentleman and, I am pleased to say, he offers me the same respect. I must show you a dagger he gave me, a work of rare price which will comfort me in my old age with tender memories of when I was young.'

'I'd like to meet him,' said Clarice. She looked at Corville.

'Have you ever seen him?'

'Yes.'

'Is he as the Colonel says? Tall and handsome and proud?'

'The last time I saw him,' said Corville deliberately, 'he had just knifed a man. He then showed his pride by ordering the deaths of some twenty helpless men. If such actions make him a gentleman, then I do not wish to be classed with him. Therefore, like Captain Gerald, I am no gentleman.'

He blinked at the colonel, half aware that the closeness of the room and the richness of the unaccustomed wine was going to his head. 'Do I walk out or are you going to throw me out?'

'Silence!' Marignay was white with

anger. 'I'm surprised at you de Corville. To act and speak so in front of my guests!'

'Yes,' said Corville. 'I'm sorry. I should have known better than to speak the truth. They may want to cling to their illusions a little longer.' Suddenly he laughed. 'Sorry. I must really apologise, The Colonel is right.'

'He was found wandering in the desert suffering from thirst and heat,' explained the colonel rapidly. 'I had hoped that he had made a full recovery but apparently I was wrong. You must excuse his conduct.'

'But did he see this Sheik, what's his name, kill those men?' Dick narrowed his eyes as he stared at the young officer. 'He doesn't look sick to me, a little drunk perhaps, but not sick.'

'Of course he did not,' said Marignay. 'The whole thing was but a figment of his imagination. El Morini is a gentleman and would never do such a thing.' The Colonel touched his temple. 'The sun, you know, it can do strange things to a man dying of thirst.'

'And wounded too.' Clarice gently

touched the strip of plaster across the young man's forehead. 'How did that happen?'

'It is nothing,' said Corville, already ashamed of his outburst. 'The Colonel is right. I did suffer from too much sun and it may have left me a little light-headed.' He reached for his glass, then added:

'When did you say you were returning to Sidi bel Abbes?'

'We're not,' said Dick. 'From here we're going by camel caravan to Marojia. From there we hope to pick up transport to Toulon, then up through France, to London where we leave Miss Carson, and so back home to the States.' He stretched. 'Personally, nice as it has been to come here and see all these things, I shan't be sorry to get back home again.'

'And you?' Corville smiled into the eyes of the young woman. 'Will you be glad to leave?'

'I don't know,' she said softly. 'I'd like to stay but a woman can hardly stay in a fort on her own, can she?'

'No.'

'Tell me,' she said absently. 'What

happens when you people marry? You do marry I suppose?'

'Sometimes. Then, if the man is an officer and wise, he resigns his commission. If he is a man he doesn't get married, he can't — or if he does, then it is his own fault. The desert is no place for women, white women that is, not when every moment is filled with danger.'

'I'd wondered about that.' she said. 'The danger I mean. Tell me, is it really as dangerous as some people make out? We've not seen any trouble and we've travelled hundreds of miles across the desert. Is it all rumour or do you actually fight real battles?'

Corville thought of Le Farge and his ever present fears. He thought of blood-stained sand and the bodies of twenty legionnaires lying in their shallow graves less than half a day's march away. He thought of Sheik El Morini and the man's cold, calculated cruelty. He thought of Fort Hollendoft and what had been found there. He remembered that she was young and a guest and not really interested in the answer at all. Looking into her eyes he smiled and lied with easy skill.

'No.'

'I thought not. That Captain, Captain Gerald I think his name is, he kept trying to get us to leave sooner than we had planned.' She laughed. 'The caravan is due in five days time and there isn't any way we could leave until then so I don't know what he was worried about anyway.'

'He is a good soldier,' said Corville abruptly. 'He meant well.'

'He frightened me,' complained Miss Carson. 'He is so rough, so uncouth.' She frowned. 'De Corville,' she murmured. 'I wonder? Tell me, young man, did you go to school in England?'

'I did.' Corville was deliberately rude. The last thing he wanted was for anyone to pry into his personal history. Miss Carson nodded.

'I thought that I recollected the name. A friend of mine, perhaps you know him? Mr. Smithers? No? Well, he sent his son to the same school. At least I think that it was the same. He was telling me of a boy who was there years ago, the son of Lord Trehern.' She frowned again. 'Of course it's so long ago now but it seemed that there was some sort of scandal, I never did know what it was all about and my friend, Mr. Smithers, he had to take his boy away because he lost most of his money in a share deal or something that this Lord Trehern had floated. I did hear that the boy, he was older than my friend's son, of course, went to live with his mother in France. I . . . ' She broke off at the expression on Corville's face. 'Is anything the matter?'

'No. You were telling me of this Lord Trehern?'

'Yes. Well rumour had it that he ran away and hid somewhere.' She tittered; the wine had obviously taken effect. 'Some say that he joined the Foreign Legion, but then they always say that, don't they. It just struck me because of the name de Corville, it's an unusual name but it couldn't be the same one, could it?'

'Hardly,' said Corville drily. 'If my father was an English lord then I should know it.'

'But your English is so perfect,' insisted

Miss Carson. 'I knew that you must have been to school in England the moment you spoke.' She tittered again and, as she reached for her glass, managed to spill a few drops of the red wine on the spotless napery. Dick Mason smiled at Corville and shrugged. His sister, sensing the young officer's feelings, rested her hand with friendly warmth on his arm. Marignay, oblivious to all the byplay, grunted as he reached for a fresh bottle of wine.

'Come. Let us not be sad or remember the past, or think too deeply of the future. Let us drink to my Villa near Toulon and the wines I shall drink there and the toys, similar to the dagger I mentioned, I shall have to while away my lonely hours.' He poised the bottle over Miss Carson's glass. 'Wine?'

'I shouldn't really,' she simpered. 'I'm not used to wine and I'm afraid that it's affecting me a little.' She watched him pour her glass full. 'Only a little then and after that I'm off to bed. I always say that there's nothing like a . . . ' She broke off, her glass half tilted to her mouth, her eyes wide and suddenly strained. 'What's that?'

'Nothing,' said Marignay. 'The wind perhaps?'

'Silence!' Corville rose from the table, his stomach knotted with apprehension. Thinly through the thick walls, filtered by the embrasures and echoing from the hills around came the sound of the sentry's harsh challenge.

'*Qui va la?*'

He was answered by a shot, his scream mingling with the sound of gunfire and as he screamed both shots and cries were drowned in an undulating yell.

'*Allah il Allah! Mohamed ill akbar!*'

The attack had begun.

6

Attack

For a moment no one moved then, as the frenzied yelling slashed again through the tropic night, Corville lunged towards the door.

'What is it?' asked Clarice, her soft brown eyes wide with apprehension. 'What is that yelling, and those shots?'

'An attack.' Corville reached the door just as it burst open and Captain Gerald staggered into the room. He was sober, stone cold sober, and his eyes as they stared at Marignay were wild and flecked with blood. He had lost his kepi and his uniform was stained with an ugly splotch of spreading blood.

'You,' he said, and pointed towards the Colonel. 'You did this.'

'Nonsense!' Marignay licked his thin lips with a nervous gesture. 'Probably some tribesmen trying to gain credit by attacking the fort. They will break and retreat at the first charge.'

'You think so?' Gerald sneered and spat a mouthful of blood. 'The hills are alive with raiders. The fire from their guns makes the night seem like day. Men died where they stood, the watchtower guard, the sentries, others.' He swayed and his grimed hand fumbled with the pistol in his belt. '*Cochin! Je vous mort pour . . .* ' He staggered again his mouth filling with blood before he could finish the threat, and, as Corville reached out to steady him, the Captain fell lifeless to the floor.

Miss Carson screamed. She stood her eyes wild, her hair disarranged, and shrieked at the unaccustomed sight of freshly spilt blood. Clarice moved to comfort her and Dick, his face white and drawn, looked at Corville.

'Is it bad?'

'Yes.'

'Can I help?'

'Stay with the women. See that they stay away from the embrasures and out of the line of fire.' Corville stepped over the dead man. 'I must see what has happened. I'll return when I've learned the state of things.' He looked at the sobbing woman and gestured towards the wine. 'Give her a drink, slap her if you have to, but make her keep silent.' He was gone before the American could do more than nod.

Outside, beneath the glowing stars and the swollen moon, the night had turned into a flame-lit hell.

Bullets whined like bees over the scarred merlons, whining as they ricochetted or making a soggy thud as they ploughed into soft and yielding flesh. The fire was the heaviest that Corville had ever experienced and as he squinted at the winking points of light, he swore with an unusual savagery.

'Machineguns!'

'Two of them.' Sergeant Smith, his face grimed with sweat and dirt, squatted beside the lieutenant as he stared towards the surrounding hills. 'Spandaus I reckon, or maybe they've managed to get hold of a couple of Vickers. Whatever they are they're bad.'

'The caravan,' said Corville sickly. 'The

machineguns must have been among the load. Sacre! I could have stopped all this.'

'You could have died,' agreed the sergeant, 'but I doubt if you could have stopped it.' He pointed towards the moonlit desert as he gave a quick explanation of what had happened. 'They must have crept to within the very shadow of the walls before opening fire. They have all the cover they need while we are illuminated by the moonlight. The first shot killed the watch-guard, and it was followed by a volley that killed most of the sentries. Before we could beat them back they had dug themselves in, too close for comfort, and those damn machineguns are sweeping the walls.' He stared over his shoulder. 'Where the hell is the Captain?'

'Dead.'

'And the Colonel?'

'He'll be out soon.' Corville spat into the darkness. 'He has his guests to worry about.'

'Guests?'

'Didn't you know?' Corville looked at the bleak face of the sergeant. 'Three of them, two women and a man.' He shrugged. 'The man can fight, most Americans know how to use a rifle, but the women . . . '

'They can act as nurses.' Smith ducked as lead chipped dried brick from the merlon behind which he crouched. 'Your orders, sir?'

'Let them waste their ammunition as long as they wish.' Corville squinted into the darkness. 'We can't see them as well as they can see us, but we have thick walls and they can do us no real harm. When they charge we must be ready to beat them back.' He looked down the line of waiting men, each with his loaded Lebel, his bayonet at his side and his water canteen to hand. The dead lay where they had fallen, stiff and cold in the pale light of the setting moon. 'Release the prisoners from the cells, arm them, and have them issue a half-litre of wine per man. Relieve one third of the men at a time for food and rest and tell the others to stay behind cover. Time enough to return the fire when they have something to shoot at.'

'Yes, sir.'

'Have you any idea as to who is behind this, sergeant?'

'I'd guess at the Sheik El Morini, sir. He has been much about the fort and knows our defences too well.' Smith glanced towards the well in the centre of the compound. 'Shall I draw water, sir?'

'Can you?'

'I think so. The walls should protect me from the machinegun fire and the fort is so built that the well is protected from direct aim.' He hesitated. 'I think that it would be best, sir, wounded men need water and when the sun rises . . . '

He broke off but Corville knew what he meant. Beneath the torrid sun men's bodies craved for water as for nothing else and, during the long hours of siege ahead, water would be as essential as bullets. He was about to give the order when Colonel Marignay joined them.

'Lieutenant?'

'Sir!'

'How are things?'

'Under control, sir. I was about to order the sergeant to draw water and store it. You agree?'

'Unnecessary,' snapped the Colonel. 'The sergeant would be doing better by sending a man up into the watchtower. It is essential that I should know the movements of the enemy.'

'To send a man up there would be to send him to his death,' said Corville quietly. 'The hills are full of marksmen and they would cut him down before he was halfway up.'

'It is dark,' grunted the sergeant. 'What man can see in the dark?'

'You will do as I order,' snapped the Colonel, 'Send a man, the man I whipped will do, up into the tower. At once!'

'Yes, my Colonel.' Smith saluted and crawled away to send the unfortunate man up to the watchtower. Marignay stayed where he was for a moment then, as lead blasted dust into his face, returned to his quarters. Corville, in effect if not in name now full commander of the fort, squatted and stared bleakly into the night.

The attack was well planned, there could be no doubt of that. And yet, as he thought about it, something troubled him. To attack at night was against the regular custom of the Arabs. They preferred to attack by day, riding out of he desert and charging with blind ferocity at the walls of the fort. Sometimes, as at Fort Hollendoft, they succeeded in scaling the walls and winning an expensive victory. At others they were beaten back with heavy losses until their Mullah, the holy fanatic who was usually behind all such attacks, was either killed or announced that Allah had decreed the fighting ended.

But this attack showed signs of careful planning.

The use of the night for cover, the volley aimed to eliminate the sentries, the twin machineguns set so as to spray the walls and keep the defenders behind cover. Above all the lack of a charge. Corville bit his lips as he thought about it and felt his stomach tighten with apprehension. The attack had been planned by a master of warfare and he wondered what the next step would be.

He soon found out.

The man Marignay had ordered to the top of the watchtower screamed and pointed towards the gate just as the murderous fire from a score of rifles lanced in his direction. The scream died as lead smashed the helpless body to mangled ruin and, as the rolling echoes of the rifle fire died away, flame and smoke shot up from the outside of the gate. The explosion deafened the young officer, blinding him with its bout of searing fire and, as he blinked to clear his eyes from the retinal after-images, he felt sick horror at what he saw.

The gate had been destroyed.

Men lay around it, mostly clad in the blue and scarlet of the Legion but with here and there the drab white of a burnoose. Even as he stared, hearing the groans of wounded men and the shrill prayers of the dying, a rush of hate-filled Arabs lunged through the burst portal, their cries stabbing the air with searing dread.

'Allah il Allah! Allah the one true God. Allah the merciless. Death to the infidel! Kill! Kill! Kill!'

For a moment it seemed that they had won the fort. For a moment the compound was full of white burnoosed figures firing, slashing with their curved swords, stabbing with their pointed daggers. Men died then, brave men dressed in the blue and scarlet of the Legion but, as they died, they fought with the incredible desperation of despair. Lebels fired and fired and fired again. Then, their magazines empty, the legionnaires reversed their weapons and hurled themselves towards the shrieking enemy. Rifle butts thudded against the turbans, long sword-bayonets flashed and dulled with blood as the desperate soldiers fought hand to hand with the swelling tide of invaders. Men screamed and groaned as steel and lead ripped their vitals. Others laughed with the sheer excitement of combat while others muttered prayers to forgotten gods as they thrust and lunged, parried and ducked, rose to kill and be killed in turn.

Corville had flung himself forward at the first appearance of the enemy, his automatic spitting fire as he emptied it before snatching up a discarded Lebel. Hastily he fitted on a bayonet and thrust at a tall, burnoosed figure swinging a heavy scimitar. The shock as metal met metal almost made him drop the rifle then, as the Arab swung again, Corville lunged and grinned as he felt the slender blade of the bayonet slip between the other's ribs. Pausing only to jerk the weapon free he swung the butt at a snarling, bearded face, ducked as a rifle blasted towards him, and triggered his own weapon in reply, as something smashed with sickening force against his skull.

After that things took on a strange, misty unreality. Bearded faces with open, yelling mouths seemed to rise before him and to fall away without any effort on his part. Steel grated against his bayonet and once he felt the sting of a knife in his arm, but he seemed to be beyond all physical pain and fought more like a machine than a man, shouting orders, curses, swearing at legionnaires and Arab alike, his trained reflexes taking over from his numbed mind.

Finally it was over.

He staggered as he looked around him at the heaps of dead, staring at a sky that had suddenly changed from black to blue, and squinted at the ball of the rising sun where it rested over the horizon. Impossible as it seemed the fight must have lasted well over an hour and, as he stared at the bent and broken rifle in his hands, he wondered how it was that he was still alive. A voice called to him and turning, he saw the sergeant, his face blood-stained, crouching on the fire step, a rifle in his hands, two others at his side, the area around him littered with empty cartridge cases. Two dead men beside him stared at the sun with sightless eyes and a third whimpered as he tried to staunch the flow of blood from a stomach wound.

'Quickly, my lieutenant. Here before they fire into the compound.'

Hardly knowing what he did Corville climbed up to join the sergeant. He felt weak, dizzy, and the side of his face was stiff with dried blood.

'Here.' Smith passed over a canteen. 'Drink and pour the rest over your head.

You were a lucky man last night, the bullet meant for between your eyes only tore the flesh and almost stunned you.'

'You saw?' Corville gasped as the tepid water sent pain from his wound but beneath the shower his mind cleared and he was himself again. He stared at the piles of cartridge cases and at the position of the sergeant.

'You covered me,' he said. 'You sat up here and fired at everyone around me. Why?'

'In a fight a man must keep a cool head,' said Smith calmly. 'I saw what had happened to you and, calling these three whom I knew to be good shots, we sat up here and poured fire down into the compound. While you engaged them hand-to-hand they could not spare the time to shoot us down.' He looked at the two dead men and the one who was wounded. 'At least,' he corrected himself, 'not all of us.'

'I must have been half stunned from the bullet,' said Corville. 'How is the situation now?'

'We have managed to beat them back

120

from the compound but in doing so we have lost more than half our men. Now, with the gates destroyed we must concentrate on stemming a new charge.' Smith glowered at the heaps of dead below. 'I would give much to know who thought of pinning us down with machinegun fire while their sappers set and fired a charge beneath the gates. No Arab thought of that.'

'No,' agreed Corville. He stared at the line of weary legionnaires lining the parapet over the open gate. Too few to do more than beat off another such charge as last night. Far too few to withstand a siege of any length of time. Smith attracted his attention and pointed down towards the well.

'The trouble has only just begun, sir. Soon the men will need water, the wounded are already crying for it, and we can't draw water from the well without being exposed to the fire of the machineguns.' He pointed towards the rocky hills. 'I have watched them dismount the weapons and set them up so as to fire through the open gate. It would be certain death to attempt to cross the compound now.'

Corville nodded as he surveyed the area. The sergeant was right. As soon as the gates had been blown open the unknown genius behind the attack had set his rapid-fire weapons so as to cover the exposed compound. As yet they had not been used, while the attackers had filled the gate and battled with the legionnaires it would have been criminal folly to shoot down their own men, but now that the area was clear they could be used to render the compound impassable.

It was still possible to move around the fort, the high fire-platform protected by the thick merlons allowed that, but the sole source of water was the primitive well and that was in the centre of the compound. Corville felt thirsty as he looked at it, its nearness tempting him with its promise of cool comfort and liquid refreshment. He touched Smith on the shoulder.

'I must see the Colonel. Arrange for the wounded to be taken below. Relieve the men at intervals for food and rest, issue wine but no water. See that every man has plenty of ammunition and that, if possible, he has a spare rifle, fully loaded at his side.' He hesitated. 'I needn't tell you what to do if we are overrun.'

Smith nodded, his face grim. It was one of the tenets of the Legion that the last bullet should be saved for strictly personal reasons. Better death at one's own hand than the slow tortures of an Arab encampment.

Marignay was in his quarters when Corville arrived. His guests were with him, afraid, but still hopeful that the famous Legion would save them in the end. Corville ordered the women down to the barrack room where they could dress the wounds of the injured and sent Dick to help the sergeant.

Alone with the colonel he stated what was on his mind.

'Fort Onassis is doomed. We can beat back another charge, perhaps two, but heat and thirst will defeat us in the end. I would say that we have until this evening to do what has to be done.'

'And what is that?'

'All arms and ammunition must be gathered and ready for immediate destruction. No matter what happens they must not be allowed to fall into enemy hands.'

'I am aware of my duty,' said Marignay coldly. 'Are you certain of the position?'

'Yes. Whoever is behind this attack, and I'm certain that it is no ordinary Arab, is a clever man and knows just what he wants. The very fact that there have been no charges shows that he wants to avoid heavy losses. He is relying on the sun to defeat us, that and his two machineguns.'

'We will fight to the last,' said Marignay. 'I shall never surrender.'

'No one has asked you to, yet. The Arabs intend killing every living thing within the fort. They want the rifles and ammunition we have stored here and you must see that they don't get them.'

'I know my duty,' repeated the colonel. He reached for a carafe of water, then frowned as the young officer took it from his hand. 'What are you doing?'

'We have no water. This is needed for the wounded.'

Corville didn't even bother to say 'sir'.

He was disgusted with the inefficiency of the colonel, his weakness and apparent indecision. Even now, with the Arabs howling at his very gates, he didn't seem to realise the seriousness of his position.

To Marignay war was something fought between gentlemen where only the common soldier ever got hurt. He couldn't seem to realise that his life was as much at stake as that of the humblest legionnaire.

Corville left him standing by his desk, absently toying with the dagger that had been the gift of El Morini, and, still carrying the carafe, made his way down towards the wounded men. Clarice met him as he ducked through the low door.

The young girl's face was pale and strained, her dress stained with blood, her hands red with it, but her eyes revealed her courage and she even tried to smile.

'How is it going?'

'Not good.' Corville handed the carafe to Smith and called to Miss Carson. 'Here.'

'You want me?' Like the young girl Susan's hands and dress were horribly stained but, again like the young girl, she had an inner courage which made Corville proud to call her his country-woman.

'Listen.' He lowered his voice so that the wounded could not hear what he was about to say. 'If by chance, and remember I only say if, we are defeated and the Arabs should overrun the fort there is something you should know.'

'Things are serious, aren't they?' Clarice smiled at the young man. 'Don't try to lie to us. It is better that we know the truth.'

'The truth is that we shall be overrun by nightfall,' Corville said harshly. 'The men will be killed, we expect that, but you may not be treated so mercifully.' He hurried on before they could interrupt. 'When the end is near I shall hide you and your brother together with Miss Carson in one of the cells. I shall lock you in so that, when the Arabs arrive, you will have a chance to speak with them before they can kill your brother. You must say to them the following words in Arabic. It is the first sentence of the Koran and will tell them that you have embraced Islam and that you wish to accept the Moslem creed. Now, 'In the name of Allah, the merciful . . . ''

Again and again he repeated the Arabic words, drumming it into their heads until he was satisfied that they had learned them by heart. Clarice paused in her recitation and stared at him.

'Will they let us go?'

'Perhaps. They will probably hold you to ransom but, as a Moslem, you will not be tortured or unduly harmed.' He didn't think it worth mentioning that the likelihood was high that some Sheik might decide to take them into his Harem, or that Dick might be set to menial tasks. He had done the best he could to save them in emergency, and he could do no more.

He jerked his head at Smith as he left the long, low barrack room now echoing to the cries of thirsty men.

'Sergeant, what would be the chances of your getting through to Sidi bel Abbes with a message?'

'None, sir.'

'I think that you would stand a chance.

I've noticed that there are several Beni Seidel Rif adventurers and looters among the attackers. You have the same colour eyes as the Riff and I understand that you speak the Beni Seidel version of the language of the Moroccan Berbers. In disguise you could pass for a Beni Seidel. I want you to try and slip through the enemy lines and carry news of this attack and what we have learned from it to Colonel Le Farge at Legion headquarters. This is no ordinary attack. If they succeed, and it is hard to see how they can fail, then the path will be open to Marojia. Once the tribes learn that they can defeat us then they will be willing to rise to the voice of any Mullah preaching rebellion. It is essential that this news gets through to Colonel Le Farge.'

'Begging the Lieutenant's pardon,' said the Sergeant, 'but he is more suited to the task than I. You could disguise yourself as a Toureg or as a Berber and so mingle with them unsuspected. The tribesmen have no great love for the Rif adventurers and once out of the area I would hardly be safe.'

'I gave you an order, sergeant. How long will it take you to be ready to leave?'

'I am not going.' Smith stared defiantly at the young officer. 'I refuse to obey your orders. You can break me, if you will, or report me for insubordination and have me sent to a penal colony, but I will not leave the fort while you remain behind to face certain death.'

It was impossible to argue. Corville knew that, knew too that the sergeant would rather be shot than leave him alone, and, angry as he was at the man's disobedience, yet he felt strangely touched by the sergeant's loyalty. He lifted his head at the sound of bugles and stared wonderingly at the man at his side.

'Assembly? Not alert? What is happening?'

Smith shrugged and led the way up to the firing platform. To either side of them the legionnaires stood in readiness, their eyes hard as they stared down at the small party advancing towards the fort.

Corville recognised one of the men below, the tall stately figure of the Sheik El Morini, and turned as Marignay climbed slowly up the steps to join him. The Colonel was afraid, he showed it in every movement of his hands, the flickering of his eyes and the way he wiped sweat from his streaming face and neck. He swallowed as he stared down at the advancing party.

'They've asked for a parley, de Corville,' he explained. 'I thought that it would do no harm to hear what they have to say.'

'What good can a parley do? Even if you could trust them, which you can't, what's the good of words? You know what they want from us and you know as well as I do that above all, they must not have it.'

'At least let us hear what they have to say.' Marignay stared down at the Sheik as he came to a halt. 'Speak. This is Colonel Marignay, the commander of the fort who addresses you.'

'Is it so?' There was a sneering contempt in the Arab's voice and his French, while comprehensible, was of the sort acquired in the gutter. 'I greet you as a live man greets the dead. What I have to say is simple and soon done. Surrender your command, give us the arms and ammunition you have within your walls, and you and your men shall be allowed to go free. I have spoken.'

'You can't agree,' snapped Corville. He turned to the sergeant. 'Warn the men to cover that party. At any sign of treachery they are to be shot without compunction.'

'Yes, sir.' Smith hurried away before Marignay could stop him touching the shoulders of several men who, at his whispered instructions, levelled their Lebels at the Sheik and those with him.

'I must have time to think of what you have said,' shouted Marignay. 'Come again tomorrow and I will then have decided.'

'I agree, but there will be no truce. Tomorrow the time for parley may be over. But one thing I tell you. If you surrender to me the guns you hold, then your life will be spared and much gold given you. If you destroy those arms then you will die beneath the knives of my women. This I swear. In the Koran I swear it and as I have sworn so it shall be.'

He turned and walked away, a proud son of the desert and, as he vanished behind a file of rocks, Marignay wiped his perspiring face and neck.

'Do you think that he meant what he said?'

'He meant it,' said Corville grimly. 'He swore to it on the Koran and no Arab will ever break that oath.' He shrugged as he stared at the fearful face of the colonel. 'You know what to do, of course?'

He meant that the colonel should kill himself after destroying the guns so as to save himself the promised torture, but Marigany seemed to have arrived at a different conclusion.

'Yes,' he said slowly. 'I know what to do.'

Corville bit his lips with thoughtful suspicion as he stared after the figure of the colonel.

7

Escape Into Inferno

Two men died within the next hour. They died from machinegun bullets as they tried to draw water from the well. Following their deaths came the expected charge and the newborn day was rendered hideous with screaming raiders and the echoing volleys from the defenders' rifles. The legionnaires beat back that charge but, when the burnoosed figures had hidden themselves again in the hills, less than half of the remaining legionnaires were left to defend the shattered fort.

And those few had no water.

Thirst became a real and living thing, The sun, burning down from the cloudless sky, seemed to suck every drop of moisture from their veins so that they licked their cracked lips and sucked at bullets to relieve their thirst. Sergeant

Smith, his brown scarred face grimed and streaked with sweat and blood, saluted as Corville came up to him.

'The men are in bad shape, sir. We have no water at all now, what little there was has been given to the wounded, and the wine is almost all gone.'

'How is that?' Corville knew that the fort, like most garrisons, usually contained a great deal of wine. In many cases it was better to drink wine than water of doubtful purity and, in any case, the legionnaires were entitled to a ration of two litres per man per day. Smith shrugged at the officer's question.

'The casks were punctured by bullets, sir. Some of the Arabs, or it may have been sheer chance, fired at the barrels. The wine leaked out before I could plug the holes. There is a little left, a few litres only, and I have issued that to the wounded.' He stared up at the sun. 'In any case it is not good for men in the sun to drink too much wine.'

'I see.' Corville glanced at the sweat-streaked faces of the legionnaires. Below them, in the centre of the compound, the well was a mockery with its promise of endless water but, menaced as it was by the machineguns, it was a death trap.

Standing on the firing platform he stared towards the rocky hills, his eyes narrowed as he sought to locate the deadly weapons.

'What are you thinking of, sir?' Smith crouched beside him his eyes anxious.

'We must have water,' said Corville. 'Tell me, have you managed to locate the machineguns?'

'Yes, sir.' Smith pointed then drew back as a Jezail spat fire and sent its heavy slug whining towards him. 'They have one over there, behind that pile of stones. The other is to the right, see? Just behind that boulder.'

'I see them.' Corville nodded as he spotted the thick barrels and improvised defences of the two guns. 'Smith, you are a good shot. Are there many other marksmen left to us?'

'All the legionnaires are good shots, sir. But I know what you mean. Jenson, Henriques, Schwarzt and Brunner are about the best marksmen we have now.'

'Good. Get them together, each with a man to load for him, and extra rifles to hand. Place them so as to lay a cross-fire over the machineguns. Give them orders to shoot every man who tries to serve those guns and, at the command, to concentrate on rapid fire. I want to prevent those guns from being fired for long enough to get some water from the well.'

'I understand you, sir, but you will, naturally, call for volunteers to get the water.'

'I was thinking of getting it myself.'

'No, sir. With all respect to the lieutenant he must not do that. If he were killed the fort would be without a commander and . . .'

'Colonel Marignay is your commander,' said Corville shortly.

Smith shrugged.

'The men think otherwise, sir. You will permit me to call for volunteers?'

Corville nodded, there was nothing else he could do. As Smith had said he was, if not in name, then in fact in command.

The arrangements were soon made. Eight men, four to each machinegun position, took their places, each man with one other to act as his loader and to pass him a refilled weapon. Corville placed Jenson and Schwarzt with Smith and one other man, taking Brunner, Henriques, and a small, wiry Basque as his own team. Tensely they crouched behind the merlons, gauging distances and trying to forget that, even as they fired, they would be targets to the watching Arabs.

'Ready?' Corville rested his cheek against the stock of the Lebel, drawing a bead on an inch of turban showing from behind a rock. 'Let the volunteers start as soon as we open fire. Now!'

Eight rifles spat as one and an Arab, his turban splotched with red, sprang from behind his cover, shrieked a prayer to Allah, and died with four bullets in his body. Again the rifles sent echoes across the surrounding hills, again, again, the swift reports sounding almost as if the men were using machineguns instead of bolt-action rifles. Corville aimed and fired, aimed and fired until his mental count told him that he was using his last cartridge. Swiftly he threw down the rifle, lifted the loaded weapon his attendant had placed in his hand, and was firing again without a second's pause.

Splinters of rock and shattered stone flew from where the machineguns rested behind their barricades. One gun began to stutter its song of death then fell silent as lead whined towards the gunner. For a moment it seemed that the plan would succeed then, as the watching tribesmen saw what was happening, rifle fire echoed from the hills and leaden messengers of death whined through the burning heat towards the fort.

The Basque swore, stared stupidly at the sun, then toppled lifeless towards the sand below. Henriques twisted as if something had cut the nerves of his legs, screamed in a strange, high-pitched voice, then, his kepi falling from a head that was a red-stained ruin, fell towards the compound. Corville gritted his teeth as splinters of dried brick stung his cheek, fired at a turbaned head, swore as the rifle jerked almost out of his hands, and flung it down, its stock torn and his barrel bent by the heavy bullet from a Jezail. Quickly he re-aligned the new weapon handed to him, then swore with hopelessness as a machinegun began to spray the fort with lead.

'Down!' He snatched at Brunner's arm. 'Down, you fool!'

'I'll get that gunner first.' Brunner, a study in cool detachment, aimed as if he were back on his own Yorkshire Moors shooting at nothing more harmful than a rabbit. Twice he fired then, as he grunted and took more careful aim, the hosing death from the machinegun swept towards him.

Corville shuddered as he turned away from the body. Brunner had been a handsome man but now? Now his head had been literally ripped from his body and blood spouted from the severed arteries.

Smith came crawling towards the officer, his face grim as he stared down into the compound. Corville followed his gaze, half-hoping that the volunteers had managed to win a little water. His heart sank as he saw two figures sprawled beside the well.

'Snipers,' explained Smith. 'They were more clever than we thought. The machineguns were to keep us down and their own snipers covered the well.' He stared at the men who had died. 'Eight men dead and not a cupful of water in return.'

'I shall be the next to try,' said Corville harshly. 'We must have water, even a canteen would do. You can't hope to cross the desert without it.'

'I'm not crossing the desert, sir, I told you that.' Smith snatched up a rifle and fired at a distant shape. A thin scream echoed from the surrounding hills and a blob of white sprawled across the rocks. The sergeant smiled with grim humour as he reloaded his Lebel.

'That's one devil the less. I wish that they were all as easy to kill.'

'Someone must carry the news to Colonel Le Farge,' insisted Corville. 'I am in command here, I can't go. Of all the others you stand the best chance.' He gripped the sergeant's shoulder. 'Damn it, man! Can't you see how important it is?' He had lapsed into English and Smith answered in the same tongue.

'There is something else far more important, sir. There are two women in the fort, and you know what will happen to them if they are found by the Arabs. I think that it would be best to shoot them before the final charge. The brother too, it is not fair that he should have to suffer because of the criminal stupidity of the Colonel.'

'Sergeant!'

'I mean it, sir. Colonel Marignay is a dangerous fool. Worse than that. For one thing he is far too friendly with Sheik El Morini. For another, hasn't it struck you as odd that he sent a relief column out to rescue us in the desert? Did he want to rescue us? Or did he want to weaken the garrison by having more men killed before the attack?'

'Do you know what you are saying, Smith?' Corville glared at the sergeant in shocked disbelief. 'You are accusing him of being a traitor!'

'Well?' Smith stared steadily at the young officer. 'This whole attack is out of the ordinary. The attack at night, when always before the Arabs attack by day. The blowing up of the main gate and the setting of machineguns to deprive us of water. The Colonel, remember, wouldn't let me draw water for storage when we had the chance. And another thing, why doesn't he show himself more often? The men are beginning to talk. They wonder why he remains in his quarters so much, and remember, the arms and ammunition are stored beneath the Colonel's private chambers. He has the key and, without it, we can't get in to destroy them.'

'The parley,' said Corville, 'I was suspicious even then. It sounded as if El Morini was reminding the Colonel of what would happen to him if . . . ' He swore with bitter anger. 'A traitor! Is it possible?'

'Perhaps the Colonel is just weak,' suggested Smith. 'I have no proof of what I say, but this I do know. The Colonel talks of a Villa near Toulon. How can any officer afford a luxury villa? Marignay has no private means, that is why he persuaded his friends to get him this command. How did he become rich so soon?'

'So you think that Marignay will permit us all to be killed and then, when the battle is over, hand over the guns and ammunition to the raiders?'

'Yes.'

'You could be right and if you are . . . ' Again the young officer swore bitterly as he thought of what would happen if such a thing were to come to pass. Armed from the fort, inspired by their easy victory, the tribesmen would call on their brother nomads and, within days, the desert would be aflame with war. Marojia, the arsenal town of the Legion, would be attacked and fall easy prey. Then, armed to the teeth, the Moslems would declare a holy war and the Great Jehad that Le Farge feared would drench the sands of the Sahara in innocent blood.

Corville stared up at the sun, now directly overhead, than looked towards the enemy-filled hills

'Listen. This news must reach Colonel Le Farge. It is more important that he should know of the threat to Marojia than that we should try to save the fort here at Onassis.'

'The fort is doomed,' said Smith bleakly. 'It is just a question of time before we are all dead. One more charge, perhaps, and then, at nightfall without a doubt, the garrison will fall.' He glared towards the skulking Arabs. 'They are beginning to value their own skins. Why should they charge and die, even if it means taking the fort now, when they can wait until the sun has weakened us and their snipers cut down our number? If what I think is right then they will wait until nightfall to attack. Then there will be fewer of us to destroy the guns. The Colonel can make his unholy bargain with El Morini, and, no matter what tale he chooses to tell, there will be none to deny it.'

'What do you suggest?' Corville asked the question as he would ask it of an equal. The sergeant was no ordinary man and, had he wished, he could have been a captain long ago.

'The news, as you say, must be carried to Sidi bel Abbes. You must take it if, for no other reason, you will be believed where I would not. Again, you have the experience to pass yourself off as an Arab. Your features are the same, you speak the tongue like a native, and you know the religion and customs.' Smith stared at the young man. 'You must disguise yourself, await the final charge and then, in the confusion, slip over the wall, mingle with the enemy, and so make your way through their lines.'

'And desert you all?'

'Yes.' Smith glanced at the grim-faced men lining the parapet. 'Legionnaires are not afraid to die. They will fight to the last man and kill as many as they can. There is no fear that any of them will live to be tortured. But it is up to you not to have made their sacrifice in vain. Unless the news reaches Sidi bel Abbes then all the dead and those who are about to die will curse you from their graves for having failed them.'

'You are right.' Corville sighed as he thought about it. He would rather have stayed behind to have died with his men but that would have been a useless gesture. The fate of a nation depended on what he would decide and, with the scales balanced that way, he had no real choice.

'Then you will go?' Smith stared anxiously at the young man. 'You will carry the news?'

'Yes.'

'Good. I shall attend to the women. It will be better for them to die now than to fall into the hands of the Arabs.'

'Wait!' Corville swallowed as he tried to imagine the young American girl lying dead with a bullet in her brain. 'It may not be necessary. I have taught them the words of renunciation and acceptance of Islam. The Arabs will not kill them if they are true believers.'

'Normally, no, but things are not normal.' Smith scowled towards the Colonel's quarters. 'They will be killed,' he said quietly. 'If for no other reason than that they know too much. If the Arabs do win the guns and ammunition then neither Marignay or El Morini will want witnesses to what happened. Moslems or not all Ferengi will be slain. The men immediately, the women . . . ' He shrugged and Corville knew what he hinted. Again he thought of Clarice and

146

the thought of what might happen to her filled him with an inner sickness.

'Can't we save them?'

'How? Take them with you? Impossible!'

'But is it?' Hope burned in Corville's eyes. 'Listen. You can pass for an Arab and we can disguise the women and the man. Together we can slip through the enemy lines and make our way to Sidi Baba. There we can obtain transport to Sidi bel Abbes.' He gripped the sergeant's shoulder. 'We can do it, man. The five of us can escape this death trap easier than one.'

'I don't know.' Smith hesitated, torn between his loyalty to the officer and his desire to die with his comrades. 'I will admit that there is a greater chance of five of us getting through than one. We shall be better able to defend ourselves for one thing, but . . . '

'It is an order, Sergeant,' said Corville quietly, guessing the reason beneath the other's hesitation. 'We travel together or none of us travels at all.' He squinted at the sun again. 'Get the girls ready and instruct them in what to do. When darkness falls and the Arabs charge again we shall slip over the wall and away. Pray Allah,' he said fervently, 'that they do not charge before then. I do not think that the men could withstand it.'

Allah must have heard and answered his prayers. The sun swung to the horizon and still, aside from a desultory fire from the hidden snipers, the fort was quiet. Quiet that is aside from the groans of the wounded and the cravings of men tormented with thirst. Twice they had tried to draw water from the well and each time the stutter of the machineguns had made a ghastly accompaniment to the death of another man. Now the area around the well was covered with the bodies of the slain and the thick, dried brick of the inner wall was mottled with the pit-holes of bullet marks.

Corville stared grimly at the dead, knowing that soon he too must make the attempt to snatch a little water from the well. It would be tempting fate to try it, but it would be certain death for them all if he did not. To cover the distance between Onassis and Sidi Baba without water was an impossibility. They would be dead before they had covered a third of the distance.

The young officer had a plan, which, suicidal as it seemed, was the only one he could think of. It depended on speed, speed and darkness. And he waited for the all-too-short twilight that would herald the coming night and the last, final attack of the Arabs. The sun sank lower, lower and a strange hush filled the air as, obeying the call of their Mullah, the Arabs bent towards Mecca in prayer. As he heard the thin, high voice of the Mullah calling the faithful to prayer the young officer acted.

Gripping a half-dozen canteens beneath one arm he lunged forward towards the dimming shape of the well. He ran as he had never run before, trusting to the dim light, the concentration of the Arabs on their Mullah, and the very suddenness of his attempt to defeat the enemy gunners. He covered half the distance, two thirds, three quarters, and, just as he reached the waist-high parapet, a rifle bullet chipped

149

splinters from the brickwork before him. With one bound Corville jumped over the top of the parapet and, snatching at the bucket-rope with his free hand, dropped down to the liquid coolness below.

Quickly he filled the canteens, then, laving his face and body, drank his fill of the crystal clear water. Slinging the canteens around his chest he gripped the bucket-rope and climbed towards the top of the well. At the top, just below the parapet, he halted, his heart thudding against his ribs as he faced the most dangerous period of his attempt.

All the other attempts had failed because the men had been cut down before they could raise the water. He had solved that problem by jumping down into it but now, with his mission almost completed, he still had to get out of the well and behind the safety of the thick walls. The moment he climbed from the shelter of the brickwork he would be the target for the concentrated fire of many guns. His only hope lay in speed.

From his waist he took a folded square of white material, the sun-cover of his kepi, and threw it high in the air and away from the direction he intended to go. Immediately every rifle in the fort blazed fire towards the Arabs, as the legionnaires, obeying the sergeant, fired blindly into the night. As they fired, Corville, using all the strength and agility of his youthful body, sprang out of the well and raced across the compound.

In the night the machineguns stuttered their song of death and bullets, some tracer, lanced towards him.

He stopped, ran, jumped sideways, reversed direction and then, before the gunners could swing their heavy weapons, ran full speed for the shelter of the wall.

He made it with a scratched calf and two canteens spilling water from twin bullet holes. Even as the sergeant caught him and relieved him of his burden the night was split with the undulating yells of the Arabs as, maddened with rage at the young officer's escape, they surged to the attack.

'*Allah il Allah! Mohamed ill Akbar!*'

'Hurry.' Smith, already disguised as a Beni Seidel Rif adventurer, grasped the officer's arm and led him to his quarters. 'The women and the man are ready, I've told them all to keep silent no matter what the provocation. The women are supposed to be your wives, the man a dumb lunatic and you'll be an itinerant Berber. As a lunatic the Arabs will think the American 'a ward of Allah' and he will be safer than if he carried a couple of machineguns.' The sergeant paused, fighting his desire to grab a Lebel and join in the fighting. 'Hurry!'

Quickly Corville stained his face and body a deeper brown, donned the loose burnoose and turban of a Berber, strapped a belt containing a long, thin-bladed dagger around his waist and picked up a Lebel. The rifle could be explained by a raid on a fort, too many Arabs boasted of the possession of similar rifles and were an object of envious pride to their fellows. Beneath their burnooses both Smith and Corville strapped a pair of automatic pistols, thrusting extra clips into hidden pockets inside the loose garments. A heavy camel whip and a curved sword completed their attire.

Corville paused as a fiendish yell rose above the firing of the rifles and stared at the sergeant.

'They're in the compound. The devils!' His hands clenched at his own helplessness. 'Hark at them.'

'Ready?' The sergeant looked up from where he had poured the contents of the canteens into a water container made from the sewn skin of a goat. 'Let's get away from here.'

He spoke sense and Corville knew it. It was useless to blame himself for deserting his men. He had a higher duty and to die would be the easiest thing to do. He gritted his teeth as he heard a man scream with indescribable torment and, just as a fresh wave of yelling Arabs beat down the last of the defenders, he, together with the sergeant, the American and the two women, slipped over the far wall and, crouching between the rocks, made their cautious way through the enemy lines.

That they succeeded at all was wholly due to the fact that every Arab in the vicinity was hastening to the fort to be in at the kill. They paid no attention to the little group. Their minds filled with greed for rifles and ammunition.

As Corville and his party mounted the summit of the surrounding hills the red fire of burning blossomed from the doomed fort.

Resolutely Corville led the way into the trackless desert.

8

Ali Ben Sirdir

The journey to Sidi Baba was, even in the best of times, not one to be undertaken lightly. Between the fort and the Arab town stretched miles of barren desert without a single waterhole or oasis to refresh the weary traveller. Now, on foot, with scant water and with three people unused to desert conditions, Corville at times doubted whether or not they would succeed or leave their bones to whiten on the burning sand.

Three days after leaving the doomed fort he knew that, as things were, they would never make it. Alone he and the sergeant could have won through but the women, especially the older Miss Carson, weakened fast beneath the twin perils of thirst and sun. At evening camp Smith called Corville to one side and spoke to him in a low tone.

'The women can't make it, sir. The man is doing his best and may pull through but his sister, despite what she says, can't go on much further.'

'And the other one, Miss Carson?'

Smith shook his head then, as Clarice came towards them, began to speak in Arabic.

'One day more. Then she will either have to be carried or die.'

'Talking about me?' Clarice smiled at the two men. Beneath her thick veil her face was strained and revealed her weakness and Corville knew that as things were she would die before reaching the Arab town. He looked helplessly at the sergeant then, as Clarice continued to stare at him, forced himself to smile.

'We were saying that it wouldn't be long before we arrived.'

'Is that true?' Clarice shook her head. 'Don't bother to lie to me. We're in trouble, aren't we? If you didn't have us along you'd be able to make much better time. And the water, that isn't going to last out either, is it?'

'It will last,' said Corville, but he didn't

mention that it wouldn't last more than another day, and even then he and the sergeant had given their shares to the women. Clarice stepped up to him and gripped his hands.

'I guess that I haven't had a chance to thank you for saving our lives yet. Now I want you to know that I appreciate all that you've done for us. One day, perhaps, I'll be able to show you just how grateful I am.'

'Forget it.' Corville squinted at the sun and nodded to the sergeant. 'Well, we may as well push on while it's cool. If we travel at night and avoid the heat of the day we won't suffer so much.'

Tiredly they fell into step and began the long, monotonous march towards the distant town. It was sheer slogging footwork, up one swelling dune to the crest, and then down the other side. They walked through a wilderness of sand, marching across what appeared to be a frozen sea without as much as a blade of grass to break the eternal emptiness. They walked like things of wood, their legs numb from constant effort, their tongues swollen from lack of water and their muscles weak from lack of food. On and on, fighting a desperate race against time, against the time when they would fall and be unable to rise again. Corville remembered his own recent experience in the desert and shuddered to think of the same fate befalling the young American girl. As he marched he found himself thinking more and more of her, how soft her eyes were, how sweet her lips, how nice it would be to lounge beside her on some cool seashore with the murmur of the waves reaching their ears and the cool, so cool spray dashing against their faces.

He stumbled and became aware that Smith had halted the little party.

'What is it?'

'Something ahead, sir. A camp, I think.'

'A camp?' Immediately Corville was wholly alert, his wound-induced weakness forgotten as he realised what the sergeant had said. 'Toureg?'

'I don't know. It may be a party of the raiders making for Sidi Baba, or then again it could be a nomad tribe or even a camel caravan.' The sergeant looked thoughtfully at the young officer. 'Shall we take a look?'

'Have we any choice?' Corville glanced to where Clarice supported the almost fainting Miss Carson, herself supported by her brother. He lowered his voice. 'We can't go on like this another day. We'll have to chance our reception at his camp. Maybe we'll be lucky but if they recognise us . . . '

He let his voice fade into silence but the sergeant understood. Death was a better fate than that the women should be taken and sold on the slave block at one of the mysterious towns of the deep interior.

Corville raised his voice and spoke to the others.

'Listen. There's a camp ahead of us. I do not know whether we shall be received as friends or as enemies. Remember that, under no circumstances, are you to speak. You, Dick, are supposed to be insane. You can mumble if you like but be careful not to say anything you should not know. You two women are my wives. We are a small party travelling to Sidi Baba. Leave the talking to me and do not display any curiosity.' He nodded to the sergeant. 'Right. Let's see what happens next.'

The camp was a small one consisting of a few tents, some horses, and a couple of pack camels. Corville walked directly towards the solitary guard who, as he saw the strangers, called out and levelled his Jezail at the young officer.

'Peace be with you,' greeted Corville sonorously. 'Where is your Sheik?'

'Sheik Ali ben Sirdir is within his tent,' growled the guard. 'Who seeks to disturb his rest?'

'A traveller who, with his servant, his wives, and one who is the ward of Allah has been grievously beset and robbed of his camels.' Corville lifted his hand and cursed the non-existent robbers with the full fury of outraged virtue. 'May Shaitan visit them in darkness and may dogs despoil their graves. May their sons bay at the moon and their daughters all be barren. May their wives spit in their beards and . . . '

'Peace,' laughed the guard. 'Indeed

thou curseth with the full fervour of an old man.' He gestured towards a camel-hair tent. 'The Sheik is within. If you be as you say then he will comfort thee.' The Jezail lifted. 'In the name of Allah . . . '

Corville sighed with relief as they passed the watchful guard. They had stumbled on one of the small, nomadic tribes who, unlike the warring bands, lived humbly and quietly, glad of the protection of French law. Later, when the women and the supposed 'ward of Allah' had been fed and given tents in which to sleep, Corville and the sergeant dined with the old Sheik Ali ben Sirdir.

It was not the normal hour for dining but, deeply steeped in religion as he was, the Sheik insisted on the rites of hospitality and, waking his cooks, had them prepare a great platter of cous-cous, mutton, rice, with dates and sweet sherbert to follow. Both men ate greedily and, to show their appreciation, belched mightily. The Sheik smiled and, clapping his hands, had his servants clear away the feast. A hookah was brought and, as they puffed at the water-cooled smoke, the

Sheik questioned his guests.

'Your camels were stolen, you say?'

'Aye,' said Corville bitterly. 'Three of the finest camels I ever hope to see. One was a veritable queen of the desert, of pure stock and with eyes like pools of limpid water.' He muttered a curse in Arabic. 'Gone now. Stolen by the Children of Hell.' He watched the Sheik closely as he mentioned the dreaded Touregs and, to his relief, the old man nodded.

'Terrible are the Veiled Ones,' he said. 'Harsh are they to all who come their way.'

'Allah is wise,' said Corville. 'Allah is all merciful.'

'Allah is all-knowing,' agreed the Sheik. He puffed for a while in silence. 'From whence came you?'

'Marojia. I was taking the unfortunate one, the ward of Allah, to his people at Sidi bel Abbes. We were attacked a short distance from Onassis and left to wander like dogs in the desert. Not even a camel did they leave me, but took them all and, in exchange, gave me this Ferengi rifle.'

Corville picked up the Lebel. 'Why should they do this, father?'

Thus appealed to the old man expanded with his superior knowledge. Not for one moment did Corville let himself be deceived by the affability of the Sheik. The man was friendly and religious but, if ever he learned that he had been made a fool of, his vengeance would be terrible. To the proud sons of the desert a man was what he appeared to be and, if he was false in that claim, then he would be treated with contempt, disdain, and, in the case of unbelievers, with torture too horrible to think of. So, as Corville listened to the old man, he did not make the mistake of revealing his true identity. Instead he withdrew even further into his disguise, finally managing to think wholly like the Arab he pretended to be, a trait that had made him one of Colonel Le Farge's most valued operators.

'I have heard these whispers,' he said when the old man had paused. 'In the bazaars men speak of the Great Jehad and of war flaming in the desert and of strange men who have come among us with strange skills so that the walls of Ferengi fortresses crumble as if at the touch of a Djinn. And yet . . . ' He paused with calculated hesitation. 'I have lived in peace with the Ferengi. At Marojia and at Sidi bel Abbes I have traded with them and always found them fair to deal with. Why must so many die to sweep them into the sea?'

'Speak not so in the tents of the Toureg,' said the Sheik warningly. 'Nor in the encampments of the Bedouin. Such words will cause you to be flayed and staked on an anthill. And yet, old as I am, and one who has seen his share of war, your words have the ring of truth. Now we can tend our herds in peace. We can trade with the white-skinned Ferengi from far away and our chests are lined with gold from the sale of our horses and rugs. Want no longer comes among us and because of that, we are able to gain credit with Allah by the exercise of charity.' The old man paused and sucked reflectively at his hookah. 'When I was a boy only a few could make the pilgrimage to Mecca and a Hadji was a man of reverence. Now, because of the Ferengi, all can make the sacred journey and all who are true in faith should do so.' He looked pointedly at Corville's unmarked turban and touched the green thread in his own.

'I have two wives,' muttered the young officer defensively. 'But in ten moons I was to make the journey to kiss the Kabaala. Now, because of those dogs who robbed me, the pilgrimage will have to wait for a further thirty moons. Allah knows that I long to make the pilgrimage, but what would you? With hungry wives and an afflicted one to take care of, not to speak of small sons of distant cousins who must be fed . . . ' He spread his hands in despair. 'Allah smite the dogs for what they have done to an honest man.'

'What is written is written,' said the Sheik severely. 'All things are as God wills.'

'Allah is all-knowing,' replied Corville, recognising the fatalism of the East. 'But even a dog can bay at the moon.'

'And a jackal can snarl at a lion,' said the old man good-naturedly. 'But come, we talk of the past. What of the things yet to come? Whither are you bound?'

'Sidi Baba. I was to sell my camel there, what a creature! But now I must beg charity until I reach home again.'

'Perhaps I could help you,' said the Sheik slowly. 'I linger here for a while then move south to meet the young men of my tribe who are catching wild horses in the hills. After they are broken we make our way to Sidi Baba and from there to Sidi bel Abbes where we hope to sell the beasts to the Legion Etrangere. The Ferengi pay good gold for good beasts.'

'You sell to the Legion?'

'Why not,' said the old man calmly. 'I have listened to the Mullah known as the Hadji Hassan but find his words of air and idle promise. If he had his way he would spill the blood of the faithful in a desire to overthrow the French rule. But Allah knows that we of the desert do not wish to live in towns. What need then to sweep the Ferengi into the sea? Let them rule if it so pleases them and, as for us, we hunt and war, fight and tend our herds, live as our fathers lived and die as they die. It is the will of Allah.'

It was also good sense and Corville's respect for the Sheik grew as he listened. Ali ben Sirdir knew truth when he saw it and, as he said, the tribesmen did not really want to rule the coast. They lived as they had always lived, a nomadic life in the desert that was their home and their own special territory. War between the tribes was, to them, a game. Clear thinking men knew that once the French had been swept away other, perhaps worse systems of government would take their place. Morocco, without the Legion to both police and defend it, would be an easy plum for the picking by greedy powers who, once in command, would destroy the Arabs as a nuisance.

'This Hadji Hassan,' said Corville. 'What manner of man is he?'

'A renegade. A Ferengi who has embraced Islam. A man from the far North who has advised certain Shieks on how to make war and has taught them the use of arms. A trouble-maker who preaches the Jehad and yet who lies in his throat at the same time. A dangerous fool who other fools follow and will, with him, find Shaitan waiting at the end of the road.'

'I see.' Corville nodded. It was as Le Farge suspected, a foreign power had sent an agitator into Morocco to stir up the ever-restless natives. With gold and modern weapons he had bribed the loot and power-hungry Sheiks of whom El Morini was the leader, to revolt and unfurl the banners of war. The trouble was that nothing succeeds like success and with Fort Onassis a burned ruin, Marignay a possible traitor, and the path to Marojia open to the newly-armed hordes, peace in the desert was something almost totally lost. Corville bit his lips to hide his impatience. The news had to get to Le Farge but without the aid of the old Sheik he was powerless to move, He could not, dare not leave the two girls and Dick in the grasp of the Sheik.

Once the old man guessed that they were not what they appeared he would kill them to avenge the insult given by accepting his hospitality. The only thing

168

Corville could do was to stay with the Sheik until they reached Sidi Baba, and from there try to get transport to Sidi bel Abbes.

He mentioned the matter as delicately as he could.

'I have no spare horses,' said Ali ben Sirdir, 'and no one to escort you even if I had. My guards I need for, with the desert aflame, not even Allah could protect me or mine should the Veiled Ones sweep down on me.' He looked speculatively at the Lebels both Corville and Smith carried. 'They are good weapons you bear.'

'Ferengi guns.' Corville reached for his rifle and passed it over to the Sheik. 'I am not the beggar I seem, Mighty One. If it will please you to accept a small token of my regard, a mere nothing, but something which, at the most may serve to amuse you for an idle hour, take it with the blessings of Allah that your aim be always true.'

'It is a fine weapon,' murmured the Sheik and Corville knew that he was envious of the rifle. 'And yet I cannot take a man's weapons and leave him naked to his foes. Here.' He reached behind him and produced a Jezail. It was, in itself, a work of art with its delicate stock, flintlock action and chased barrel. The stock was heavily ornamented with precious metal and the foresight was a small but valuable pearl. Corville took it, running his hands over it, knowing that, in mere intrinsic worth, the Jezail was worth ten Lebels.

He passed it to Smith, took the sergeant's rifle, and handed it to the Sheik. Silently he spilled a double handful of cartridges onto the rug on which they sat, added more from the sergeant's bandolier, and pushed the gleaming pile of brass and lead to the centre of the carpet.

The Sheik nodded, took a powder horn and bag of bullets from a peg, and passed them to Corville. The trade made, both men sat back and smiled. The Sheik clapped his hands and ordered coffee and, over the tiny cups of strong brew, discussed future plans.

Corville knew, that by his gift of the

two modern rifles, he had in effect paid for both the hospitality and future aid. To have put such a transaction into words would have insulted the Sheik beyond redemption, but the token exchange of gifts had done more than offers of gold, haggling, or threats could ever have done.

'It will be at least a moon before we can return to Sidi Baba,' said the Sheik conversationally. 'My men will need time to break the horses. From the town we shall go to Sidi bel Abbes as I have said. Say ten days at the town, perhaps less, but not under five.' He sipped at his scented coffee. 'You may stay with me until we reach Sidi Baba.'

'You are too kind,' murmured Corville. 'As I said I am not wholly a beggar and, if you are ever in Marojia, my house is yours to do with as you please.' He hesitated.

'I fear to ask what is in my heart for fear that you would think that I ask too much, but, should things work out so and Allah direct my footsteps or the footsteps of my servant towards the city of the Ferengi, would it be possible to crave your protection to Sidi bel Abbes?'

'If Allah so wills then all is possible,' said the Sheik enigmatically and clapped his hands for more coffee.

Later, after the final cup of coffee, when they were alone for a brief space, Corville had time for a few words with the sergeant.

'We're in luck, Smith, but this will delay us and the news. It will be at least a month before we reach Sidi Baba and much could happen in that time. Anyway, should we fail to provide our own transport, I think that the Sheik will permit us to travel with him.' Corville yawned, suddenly conscious of a terrible fatigue. 'I must rest. Allah be with you.'

'Allah give you strength,' said Smith with a trace of humour and, when Corville entered the tent to which he was led, he knew why.

A startled exclamation came from the darkness as he entered and, in the thin moonlight filtering through the tent flap, he saw the pale face of Clarice staring at him with Miss Carson standing in a defensive attitude nearby. Quickly he dropped the flap and, fumbling in the darkness, moved close to the two women.

'Silence,' he rasped as Clarice made as if to speak. 'It is I, Corville.'

'But?'

'Silence.' He waited a moment until the guard had moved away. 'Listen. You are supposed to be my wives and, to these Arabs, that is just what you are. I shall have to sleep in the same tent as you do.' He grinned at the young girl's indrawn breath. 'Don't worry. Miss Carson can chaperone you, but there is nothing else I can do. One other thing. You almost spoke as I entered the tent. That must not happen again.'

Rapidly he told the two women what had transpired between him and the Sheik.

'So we are going to be together for at least a month. It will be a boring time for the pair of you because you will have to stay confined all the time. Luckily an Arab's wife is his chattel and, if I so order, no one will be surprised at Smith standing guard over you to keep outsiders away. In effect you represent my Harem, and, even as a guest, I have the right to guard you.'

'Don't bother to explain,' said Clarice gently. 'I understand.'

'Good. Remember now, on no account speak. One word from you could warn the Sheik that we aren't what we seem and, once that happens, we are as good as dead.' He hesitated. 'I'm sorry about this, it's not going to be a pleasant time for either of you, but it was the best I could manage.'

'Forget it,' Clarice whispered. 'Why not get some sleep now? You must be all in.'

Corville smiled at her in the dark, squeezed the slender fingers he found thrust into his own and, lying on a bale of soft carpets, soon fell into a dreamless sleep,

Clarice stared towards him for a long time before she too closed her eyes in slumber and when she did, there was a smile on her full, red lips.

9

Sidi Baba

Sidi Baba was a typical native town with its rows of low, blank-walled mud houses, its noisy bazaars, the markets with steaming pots of cous-cous and sickly sweets.

The Sheik Ali ben Sirdir owned a house on the outskirts next to a clump of tall palms and, over a month after the fall of Fort Onassis, Corville and his party arrived at Sidi Baba. It had been a month in which impatience had clawed at him like a living thing, for, after they had joined the group of horse breakers, he had listened to their tales and knew now that the threat of the Great Jehad was no idle worry. The young men had been full of it, as they spoke around the campfires. Corville had seen the gleam in their eyes as they spoke of the collapse of Fort Onassis, Fort Deauville, Fort Sheimen, and of the surprise attack and battle which had wiped out two columns of Spahis, the famous camel corps of the Legion.

It had been a time, too, of growing intimacy with the young American girl and, despite all the worry of duty and the grim knowledge that, unless the news could be carried to Sidi bel Abbes, the lives of no unbelievers were safe, yet the young officer found himself thinking more and more of the sweet face and little figure of his supposed 'wife'. Miss Carson too had proved to be full of courage and Dick, acting the part of a man touched with insanity, had slowly learned enough Arabic to be able to follow a simple conversation.

The old Sheik offered Corville the sanctity of his house during his stay at Sidi Baba and Corville knew that the women would be safer with the old man than wandering the streets with him and the sergeant. Thanking the Sheik, Corville arranged to leave the women and Dick under his protection while he and Smith went out into the streets to learn what they could and to see if it were possible to hire horses or camels for the journey.

'There's something in the air,' said Smith as they walked through the streets. 'Notice the unusually large number of mounted men and see? One of the Cleuh tribe, they never come this far away from their own hills normally.'

A water seller, bowed like a beast of burden beneath the swollen skin of water on his back, passed them, clinking his brass cups and calling his wares. Corville stopped him, buying two cups of water and, as he and the sergeant drank, questioned the water seller,

'I am but newly arrived at Sidi Baba,' he said. 'It was many moons since I was last here and yet, if memory serves me well, there did not seem to be so many warriors in the streets then.' He sipped at the water. 'Has some great Sheik set up his camp at the oasis?'

'Art thou touched by Allah that thou does not know what is forwarned?' The water seller, a wizened old man, grunted as he eased his burden. 'Never before have I seen so many men in the streets and, Allah be praised, they care not what they spend. Ahmed, the sweet seller in the bazaar, is thinking of taking yet a third wife because of the gold that has recently poured into his bowl.' He chuckled and spat. 'May Allah defend him from the wiles of Shaitan . . . Two wives already and one rails at him all day for silks and fine raiment while the other is wrinkled like a date that has been left to dry in the sun. And yet, despite his burden, he thinks of taking a third wife.'

'It is written that a man should have many sons,' said Corville enigmatically. 'How is it then that all this gold is to spend? Rhamadan is long past and, even if it were so, the time of fasting would not line your pockets with gold. What great occasion is this then which makes men think of adding to their burdens with extra wives?'

'Can it be that you have not heard?' The water seller shrugged and rinsed his mouth from the skin at his back, expertly letting a stream of water gush from the brass nozzle of the water skin. 'The Hadji Hassan, the Mullah the chosen of God, the Sword of Allah, the defender of the

Faithful and the Slayer of the Infidel, is to speak at sundown. Whallah! Idle gossip will not buy bread. Allah go with you brother.'

'May you walk in peace,' replied Corville and, as the water seller turned away, his thin voice raised as he shouted his wares, spoke to the sergeant.

'Hadji Hassan is here. That would account for the gathering of the tribesmen. Something big is to happen and he is probably whipping them into a frenzy prior to the attack.' He frowned as he stared at the crowded streets.

Tall Arabs, armed with Lebels openly carried, with Sneiders, Martinis, Ross and a rare Lee-Enfield, swaggered down the streets and with them, ragged men still carrying the Jezails which had been handed down from father to son since the time when Arab craftsmen worked at primitive forges and fashioned the weapons by hand. Others mingled in the streets. Wild eyed hillmen with long swords belted around their waists, swords that had originally belonged to some adventurer who had fallen victim to the corsairs in the seventeenth century. Shaggy herders with their robes of untanned goat skin, wild as the hill men with their eyes dilated from habitual use of hashish and the knives at their belts ready to drink blood. All were attired in one way or another, all were fanatics and all walked as though they restrained themselves for the great day when they would rise and sweep the Infidels into the sea.

The wail of a Muezzin interrupted Smith's reply and, in obedience to the call to prayer, both men knelt and faced towards the East.

'Allah il Allah. Mohammed il Akbar ... There is no God but Allah and Mohammed is his Prophet . . . ' The thin voice of the Muezzin carried to all the listening worshippers and, as they bowed towards Mecca, the birthplace of Mohammed, Corville whispered instructions to the sergeant.

'We had better separate now. You wander the streets and see what information you can pick up. I'll do the same. We'll meet outside the house of Ali ben

Sirdir just before sundown. I want to hear what this Hadji Hassan has got to say for himself.'

He bowed again, and Smith grunted as the prayer ended.

An hour before sundown they met again and the faces of both men showed the strain to which they had been subject. Corville led the way out of the town and sat down beneath a palm tree.

'We're sitting on a volcano,' said Smith in Arabic. 'The whole desert is aflame with the words of this Mullah. I've never seen so many tribes gathered together at the same time. Most of them are hereditary enemies and, to see how they tolerate each other, is incredible.'

'It's dangerous,' said Corville sombrely. 'If this Hassan has managed to unite the tribes then the French won't stand a chance. The Legion will be wiped out, the colonials murdered, and it will take a full-scale invasion to restore law and order again.' He scowled towards the setting sun. 'Le Farge must know of this by now. What he doesn't know, and what I've been trying to find out, is where the main attack will be.'

'Marojia?' suggested Smith. 'The arsenal would be the logical place.'

'I know, but with the force at his command El Monini could attack and destroy any fort he wishes.' Corville shook his head. 'We've got to find out where they intend attacking so that we can concentrate our forces there and crush them for good.' He looked at the sergeant. 'Did you learn anything of value?'

'No. I met up with a couple of Riffs and we drank coffee together. They know as little as we do. It seems that El Morini has gathered the tribesmen here to listen to the Mullah, this Hadji Hassan. I think that he must be the real brains behind the whole revolt. The Sheiks are dazzled with the idea, none of them have stopped to remember that divided rule will lead to perpetual unrest and the ruin of the country. It's obvious to me that Hassan is working for some foreign power and that, if he can succeed in wiping out the Legion, they will move in to 'keep the peace'. Once that happens France will never regain her position without an all out war.'

'That must not happen,' said Corville grimly. 'So you assume that none of the tribesmen really know where the great attack is to take place?'

'Not yet, but they will know soon. They will follow their Sheiks but, at the same time, each man wants to know just what is happening and why. The reasons needn't be the correct ones but if El Morini tries to give orders without taking them into his confidence, then they will melt away and return to their own tribes. The Arab is an individual and he is proud of his independence. Loyalty to him is something he gives and can take away again. El Morini daren't chance that happening so, at sundown, I guess that Hassan will tell them where and when the attack is to take place.'

'Why at sundown, why not later?'

'The men are restless and want action. Also, the Mullah knows that the longer he waits the greater the danger of losing the element of surprise. We have agents who will learn what is happening, and he must have his own men spying on headquarters.' Smith frowned. 'I can't understand why he has waited so long. After the collapse of Fort Onassis I would have thought that they would have swept down on Marojia. Why the delay?'

'I don't know, but we can be thankful for it. That wasted month was worrying me but now it seems as if it were all for the best. If we can get word to Sidi bel Abbes as to where the attack will take place then Colonel Le Farge can arrange for more men to be sent there.' He looked at the sergeant. 'Have you managed to arrange for horses yet?'

'I have found a man who has a couple of camels for sale. I bought them, telling him that my master and his wives would be leaving soon. I . . . '

'Why did you tell him that?' Corville stared at the calm face of the sergeant. 'I can't afford to take the women with me.'

'You'll have to. The Sheik Ali ben Sirdir thinks that the two women are your wives. You know as well as I do that no Arab would leave his wives with strangers, especially without guards and servants.

Either you travel with the Sheik to Sidi bel Abbes, or you take them with you wherever you intend going.'

He was right, of course, and Corville knew it. If he intended leaving the Sheik then he would have to take the women with him. He couldn't avoid it. To try and escape without them would be to call the wrath of the old Sheik down on his head and, remembering the fast horses and young men attached to the tribe, Corville knew that he wouldn't stand a chance, Also, and more important, he daren't leave the women too long alone. They would be certain to forget some detail as to conduct or custom and, even with the training he had given them during the past month, it was a risk that he dared not take.

He stiffened as some armed Arabs walked from between the palms and strode out into the desert. Others followed them, dozens, hundreds, thousands until the entire area was a mass of armed, feral-faced men. Corville hung back so that he and the sergeant were standing at the edge of the crowd when the Mullah, Hadji Hassan, rose to speak.

He was tall, extremely tall and towered above the squatting Arabs. He was thin and, in his eyes, burned the too-bright gleam of a fanatic. Standing beside him the Sheik El Morini, together with a half-dozen other Sheiks, seemed small in comparison. A deathly hush fell over the crowd, a tense silence in which every man seemed to have stopped breathing and even the tiny sounds of weapons striking buckles, the rustle of loose garments, and the thousand tiny noises of many men died away so that the whole desert seemed hushed; and walking into that moment of crystal clear purity, the sound of the Mullah's voice echoed with startling effect.

'In the name of Allah, the all-merciful, the all wise, the all-knowing. In the name of Mohammed his prophet. In the name of the Kabaala, the Holy Stone of Mecca and in the name of the Koran, the Book of Truth. I, Hadji Hassan, greet you as brothers.'

'In the name of Allah,' breathed the crowd and the sound of their murmuring voices was as the surge of distant waves.

'How long, oh my brothers, are we to allow the infidel to spit upon our mosques and laugh in our beards? How long will the proud sons of the desert bend their necks to the heel of the Ferengi? Where is the blood of your fathers, oh Children of God? When the unbelieving dogs of the French take your tents and your rifles, strip you naked and set you on a level with the jackals of the desert, then will you raise your voice in protest, I tell you that even now the Ferengi are plotting to despoil you with their taxes and laws. I tell you . . . '

It was a masterly oration and, listening to the thin penetrating voice, Corville could guess the reaction on those around him. They did not cheer, or interrupt, that was not the Arab way, but at the end of each brief oration when the Mullah paused for breath, they gave a single shout that sent echoes over the silent sands and made the jackals howl in the far distance.

Corville looked at Smith as the sergeant tugged at his arm.

'What is it?'

'The place of attack. We must discover when and where.'

Corville nodded and, waiting his chance during a pause in the Mullah's oration, whispered to his neighbour, a gaunt-faced hill man.

'Words,' he gritted. 'Empty words. When do we grind the Ferengi dogs into the sand? I came to the gathering place for fighting not to listen to words.'

'Patience, brother,' whispered the hill man, but Corville could see that his words had taken effect. 'All will be as it is written.'

Again the Hadji Hassan spoke and again, in a following pause, Corville whispered his irritation and impatience to neighbours. And now he could see the effects of his words for, as one man whispered to another, the crowd began to grow restless and impatient. Corville saw his chance and, despite the risk, took it.

'I have travelled far, oh Hadji,' he called. 'I long to kill the unbelievers, but how can I do that while wasting my strength here at Sidi Baba. Show me the

Ferengi dogs so that I may destroy them to the Glory of Allah.'

A shout echoed his words. A deep-chested roar of approval and, as he heard it, the Mullah whitened a little then spoke to the Sheiks around him.

'Peace,' intoned El Morini. 'The time is not yet. I . . . '

'The time is now,' howled a hill man, his eyes glaring with hate. 'Death to the unbelievers! Death to the Ferengi! Death! Death! Death!'

Others took up the shout and a Berber, his mouth writhing as if he were in a fit, waved his Jezail and screamed at the top of his voice for the attack to begin — now.

For a moment it seemed as if the crowd would get out of control, maddened as it was with hate and blood lust then, as the Mullah stepped forward and raised his voice in the call to prayer, their religion calmed them and they knelt to face Mecca.

But Corville knew that the seed he had sown must blossom or the Sheiks would lose their control over the impatient tribesmen.

189

'In three days' time,' intoned the Mullah after the ritual prayers and before the Arabs could become excited again, 'the moon will be nearing its death. In the darkness of the night we shall march to the attack. Marojia shall fall and give us many guns and weapons of destruction. Marojia shall arm the faithful and, with those guns, we can sweep down on the Ferengi city of Sidi bel Abbes.' He writhed as if in a fit and froth appeared at the corners of his mouth. 'I have been granted a vision,' he shrieked. 'Lo, I stood at the foot of a mountain and beside me, shining with the grace of Allah, a tall being said unto me, 'This is the task I set you. While this mountain is here none can enter Paradise for it bars the way to righteousness. Destroy it. Sweep it aside and the Houris shall welcome those who struggle for God with open arms and warm caresses.' That mountain, O sons of the desert, was the infidel. Shall we destroy that mountain?'

Corville shouted as loud as the rest, screaming with pretended hysteria, knowing that to assume indifference was to invite comment, examination, and death. Gradually, as the Arabs screamed and cheered, he worked his way out of the crowd and back towards the shelter of the palms. Smith came with him, the scarred face of the sergeant tense beneath the strain and, as they stepped into darkness, gripped Corville's arm.

'Marojia! In three days' time they leave to attack Marojia.'

'As we expected.' Corville bit his lower lip. 'How to warn them and, at the same time, let Colonel Le Farge know where the reinforcements are wanted?' He swore as he thought about it. 'Sacre Bleu! How?'

'The Sheik Ali ben Sirdir is leaving for Sidi bel Abbes tomorrow,' said Smith. 'If . . .'

'I can't go with him,' interrupted Corville. 'If I do then you will have to come with me . . . ' He nodded and stared at the sergeant. 'Listen. You will accompany the Sheik to headquarters. Take the American with you. He is supposed to be insane and I will tell the Sheik that I am sending him there for treatment. That could be true, there is a Holy Man at Sidi bel Abbes who is supposed to have great skill in the care and treatment of those who are wards of Allah. You will go with him, both to take care of him and then to tell Le Farge what we know. I will take the women and leave for Marojia tonight. With luck I shall be able to arrive long before the tribesmen.'

'Don't rely on that,' snapped the sergeant. 'The tribesmen will travel at least twice as fast as you can, hampered as you will be with the women and slow camels. If you had horses now . . . '

'No. It would be out of character and, more important, I doubt if I could obtain enough horses to carry all we need. Horses need water and I want to avoid the water holes. With camels I can carry enough water to do the entire journey without touching an oasis. I will move slower, true, but I shall have three days' start and should be able to get there in time to warn the garrison.' His face hardened. 'The Arabs will get a surprise when they commence their night attack.

Now we know what we're up against we can more than hold our own.'

Smith nodded then frowned as he mentally calculated times and distances.

'Sidi bel Abbes is nearer than Marojia. With a forced march the reinforcements should be able to get from there to Marojia in . . . ' He bit his lip as he arrived at the answer. 'Can the garrison hold out for very long?'

'They'll hold out,' promised Corville grimly. 'Now to arrange matters with the Sheik.' He glanced at the stars. 'I'll attend to that while you collect the camels, water and food, and some rugs. Don't worry about tents, we won't need them. I want to travel as light and as fast as possible. Hurry now.'

He watched the sergeant vanish towards the town and then went to see the old Sheik.

It took the subtle bribe of a pair of automatic pistols, together with ammunition for same. It took care and appeals to religion, lies and false desperation, guile and hair-trigger matching of wits and guessing at the old man's feelings. It took endless cups of coffee, a full dinner, the ritual of feasting and the nerve-tearing restraint of impatience. It took time, five hours of time but, at the end, Ali ben Sirdir agreed to provide the sergeant and the afflicted one with some horses, an escort, and provisions for the journey to Sidi bel Abbes. More than that, he agreed, because of certain astronomical influences that would aid in the treatment of the supposedly insane man, to get him to the city as fast as possible.

This was better luck than Corville had hoped for and, as he relayed the news to Smith, he gave final instructions.

'Travel as fast as you can, make a race of it, anything, but get there. I've written a note for the Colonel so that he will know that you are to be trusted. Tie Dick in the saddle if you have to and don't forget that these tribesmen are both natural born riders and proud of their skill. Wager that you can beat them to the city, set a time limit, use your own discretion, but hurry!'

'Yes, sir.' Smith hesitated. 'And you?'

'I'll take the women to Marojia as

planned. We leave in less than an hour but I can't hasten things any faster without causing suspicion. You get away before anything happens to delay you. Get the news to Le Farge and tell him to send reinforcements to the arsenal town.' Corville slapped the man on the shoulder. 'We'll meet again when this is over and split a bottle of wine to celebrate. Alors! On route, mon vieux. Vite!'

'Yes, sir.' Smith still hesitated. 'Take care of yourself — son.'

Before Corville could reply the scarred veteran had ridden away into the night.

10

Marojia

Marojia, like Fort Onassis, was a low, thick-walled, mud-brick fortress with high parapets and the slender towers of two watch-posts rearing high above the compound. Unlike Onassis it was surrounded by the featureless desert instead of rocky hills and, guarded as it was with a full complement of legionnaires, it was considered impregnable. Here were stored the arms of the Legion, the Lebels and ammunition, the bayonets, the field mortars, the pistols and sabres for the mounted Spahis and the all too rare machineguns with their belts of ammunition.

Corville smiled as he saw it, resting on the foremost camel and twisting to smile at Clarice and Miss Carson on the other.

'See? Marojia. We've arrived in time.'

'Is that Marojia?' Clarice frowned. 'I thought that there would be a town nearby or an oasis. Surely Marojia is more than just a fort?'

'The oasis lies ten kilometres to the North together with the native town. You would have gone there had you been able to follow your original plans, but we are headed for the fort.' He goaded the camel as he spoke and they slowly wended their way down the rolling dunes towards the high gates. A harsh challenge met them just as they came within rifle range. '

'Qui vala? Who goes there?'

'Lieutenant de Corville of the garrison at Fort Onassis,' shouted Corville in French. Quickly he identified himself and the two women then waited impatiently for the heavy wooden gates to swing open. Inside the fort he breathed a sigh of relief and handed the reins of the camels to a legionnaire.

'Where is your commander?'

'Colonel Marignay is away with a company of men. Lieutenant Delmar has been left in command.'

'What!' Corville stared at the legion-naire. 'Did you say that Colonel Marignay was in command?'

'Yes, sir.'

'I see.' The young officer bit his lips then hastened in search of the lieutenant. Delmar soon explained what had happened.

'The Colonel arrived here weeks ago. He said that he had been out riding and, when he returned to Fort Onassis, he found it under attack. To save his life and to obtain help, he rode away with the Toureg at his heels. He barely managed to escape with his life. As senior officer he naturally took command. Colonel Wellman was sick with fever, he's dead now, and permitted the Colonel to take over until orders came from Sidi bel Abbes.' Delmar frowned. 'It is strange, now that I come to think of it. There have been no messages from headquarters, not even in reply to those which have been sent. The journey is long, I know, but I should have had an answer before now.'

'Your messengers are dead,' said Corville grimly. 'The desert is alive with Arabs and they will kill everyone connected with the Legion on sight.' Irritably he slammed the fist of one hand into the palm of the other. 'Sacre! How many men are left in the fort?'

'A bare company.' Delmare shrugged at the expression on Corville's face. 'What could I do? Marignay was in command and he took the rest of the men with him into the desert. He said that be had received information as to a threatened attack and wanted to forestall it by attacking the raiders before they were prepared.'

'When did he leave?'

'Three days ago.'

'I see.' Corville nodded, his mind busy with thoughts.

It was too obvious now that he had all the evidence. Marignay had obviously sold out to the Sheik El Morini, taking gold and his life in exchange for the guns and ammunition at Fort Onassis. Now, not content with what he had gained, he had taken more bribes to empty the arsenal of men so that the massed tribes would find an easy victory.

Or perhaps Marignay was more deeply involved than anyone guessed, Perhaps he had not only agreed to remain inactive, but had taken an active part in the uprising. It would be a simple matter for him to teach the Arabs the rudiments of modern war and, with his training, he could lay plans for the Sheiks to slash their way through the desert and down to the sea. Fool or not, self-seeker or merely money-hungry, Marignay was a traitor and deserved to die, but first Corville knew that Marojia had to be made safe from attack.

Quickly he informed the young lieutenant what he had learned.

'The tribes left Sidi Baba about three days after I did. They must have made up that time since then. It is imperative that we ready ourselves for an attack that may come at any moment. I have sent word to Sidi bel Abbes, but, just in case anything has happened to my messenger, you must also send the warning. Have you men you can trust who will volunteer?'

'Yes.' Delmar looked at Corville. 'We are of equal rank you and I, and yet you have had more experience in the ways of these devils. Will you take command of the fort while I, and two others, attempt to get through to the garrison at El Kish. There is a small company there and we could be back within ten days. At the same time I will dispatch two men to Sidi bel Abbes. They may get through and then again they may not. Well?'

'You are wise. The garrison at El Kish, how many men?'

'A company of Spahis. They know me and I know their officer. They would not desert their post for any other man.'

Corville nodded and, when the officer had left on his desperate journey, settled down to prepare the fort against attack. Remembering Onassis he made the men draw and store all the water they could. Before the gates, well away from the walls but near enough to be in sight, he planted crude mines made of sticks of dynamite fastened together and with a fuse leading into the fort. Other sticks he fashioned into crude bombs, then, when he had done all he could think of, he let the men rest and drink, eat and sleep as much as possible. For once in the fortress discipline was relaxed and the men, knowing what was in the wind, took advantage of the relaxation to get the sleep they would be missing later on.

The attack, when it came, followed the same pattern as at Fort Onassis.

Corville was dining with Clarice and Miss Carson, forcing himself to eat and to relax against the time he knew was coming. Clarice smiled at him, resting her hand on his and, despite his apprehensions, Corville thrilled to the touch. He was in love with the girl, he knew it, but he knew too that love had no place in his life, not until . . .

'What made you join the Foreign Legion?' Clarice smiled at the elderly woman who, taking the hint, retired to her room. 'Was it because of your father?'

'You know?' Strangely he was not displeased. It would save so much explanation. Clarice nodded.

'Miss Carson told me. She remembered you, you know that?'

'She as good as said as much at Fort Onassis.'

'Yes, and she has remembered more since then. She told me about your father, how he renounced his title and ran away.

It was a pity really, because he was not to blame for what happened. But I suppose that Lord Trehern had his pride and could not bear to be accused of company mismanagement.'

She gripped his hand. 'Are you trying to find him?'

'Yes.'

'And when you do?'

'I don't know.' He drew a deep breath, 'My mother and father separated, you know that, but she is as much in love with him now as the day they married. He could not bear to see her suffer because of what he had done. He settled what money he could on her, then, to avoid publicity, ran away. I believe that he joined the Legion Etrangers and, hoping to find him, I joined it too.'

'And have you found him?'

'I'm not sure,' he said slowly, thinking of the sergeant and of their last parting. He thought of something else too, the grim stubbornness with which the scarred man had stayed at his side and, when he had been rescued, he had a dim recollection of someone, it could have been Smith, calling him by his Christian name.

'Qui va la?' The harsh challenge was drowned by the sound of shots and, as the spiteful sound cut through the night air, the dreaded yelling of the charging Arabs made the night hideous with sound.

'Allah il Allah. Kill! Kill! Kill!'

Corville sprang from the table, snatching at his pistol and running to direct the fire from the walls. Arabs swarmed all over the desert, thousands of them, and, as the legionnaires fired and fired and fired again, it almost seemed as if they would crush the fort by sheer weight of numbers. Corville jerked a soldier away from a machinegun, cleared the stoppage with which the man had been struggling, and, traversing the heavy barrel, poured lead into the horde of white burnoosed shapes before him.

Other machineguns joined in, some falling silent as Arab snipers sent leaden death winging towards the gunners, but all resumed their stutter, sending streams of tracer bullets from the walls into the desert.

Abruptly the Arabs were gone, running towards the shelter of the dunes and the legionnaires laughed as they sent a desultory fire after them.

Corville did not laugh. Still smarting from his experience at Fort Onassis he knew that the unknown genius behind the uprising would not have sent his men to certain death without knowing what he was doing. True, more than a quarter of the garrison had died during the attack and the rest couldn't hold out forever, but, protected as they were by the thick walls, with ample guns and ammunition, they would wreck terrible havoc on the attackers before finally destroying the arsenal.

Corville frowned as he stared into the darkness. Shapes littered the desert, pale splotches in the night and, as he stared at them, he blinked and rubbed his eyes.

'Legionnaire.'

'Yes, sir?' A grinning Spaniard stepped forward and saluted. Corville pointed towards the desert.

'Those shapes down there, can you see them move?'

'Dead men move, my lieutenant? Impossible!'

'Did I say that they were dead?' said Corville harshly. 'Careful, man. Watch what you're doing!'

The Spaniard shrugged and stepping carelessly onto the firing platform, sprinted into the night. Fire winked at him, a pinpoint of red flame and, with a choked sound, he felt backwards, a red-rimmed hole between his eyes. Corville swore and shouted orders.

'Fire the fuse. Legionnaires! Fire at every shape you see, alive or dead. Vite!'

He guessed what was happening. The attack had merely been designed to cover the infiltration of the sappers. They had fallen as if shot and, when the attackers had left, had remained behind to set their charges and destroy the gates as at Fort Onassis. But for Corville the plan would have worked with similar results.

As the legionnaires fired their long Lebels at the huddled shapes below, most of their bullets hitting dead men but a few thudding into living flash, the mines Corville had laid exploded with a thundering wash of flame. Screams followed it, the shrieks of crippled and maimed Arabs and, on the sands below, broken shapes stumbled in a desperate endeavour to escape the withering fire from above.

Abruptly the night was torn with fire and lead. Four machineguns opened up from the surrounding dunes and four streams of bullets traced their fiery path towards the parapets. Men died beneath that leaden hail, cursing as they tried to silence the terrible weapons, and the firing platforms of the fort ran red with blood. Something traced a path of fire in the heavens, seemed to blossom into a luminous cloud, and suddenly the fort was brilliantly lit from a hovering flare in the sky which turned night into day.

'Very pistols,' groaned Corville. 'With those magnesium flares they can stay in darkness and see everything we do.'

Grimly he gave orders for the men to stay behind cover, crouching, unable to do the attackers any harm, while the Arabs crawled closer and closer to the undermanned fort.

And that, of course, was the trouble. One man, no matter how efficient, could only fire one rifle and cover one section of the desert. The walls were too long, the men too few, the defending fire too scanty. The Arabs could concentrate ten men to cover a single embrasure and, at the sight of a Lebel or a kepi, ten bullets would blast towards living flesh. It was only a matter of time before the Arabs swarmed over the walls.

Unless . . .

Unless Smith had managed to deliver his message to Colonel Le Farge. Unless the Colonel sent reinforcements immediately to the threatened fortress. Unless Delmar had managed to get through and was returning with his Spahis. But as the days passed and Delmar did not appear Corville knew that the brave officer had met his death in a hopeless attempt to find aid.

The fate of Marojia now depended on whether or not Smith had managed to reach headquarters in time.

Four days later the Arabs managed to swarm over the walls.

They came in a yelling crowd, firing, stabbing, hacking and killing with a frenzied blood-lust, shrieking their hate at the hated Ferengi, almost insane with religious fervour and the taste of success.

Corville withdrew into the arsenal, the two women and a handful of legionnaires all that remained of the depleted garrison. Doggedly they barricaded themselves in, firing until their weapons grew too hot to hold, hurling the crude bombs into the heart of the attacking swarm and blowing the attackers to an early Paradise. But, no matter what they did, it wasn't enough, and Corville knew that they were doomed.

Incredibly the attack ceased and, in the silence, the harsh voice of the Sheik El Morini sounded unnaturally loud.

'Hear me, Ferengi. Surrender and your lives will be spared.'

'Like Marignay's?' Corville pressed down the rifle a man held and who was just about to shoot the speaker.

'Aye. He is rich with Arab gold and, if he obeys me, he will have a high place in affairs yet to come.'

Morini laughed without humour. 'Much has he taught us and much has he done. Be like him. Embrace Islam, surrender the arsenal, aid us in the Great Jehad, and your lives will be spared. By the beard of the Prophet I swear it.'

Corville hesitated. Not on his own account for, to him, surrender was unthinkable, but he had two women in his care and, if by some way he could manage to save them, then that way had to be found. Clarice must have guessed what was in his mind for she came up to him and shook her head.

'No, dear. You can't betray yourself for me. If we die, then we die together.'

'Your answer?' El Morini seemed impatient. 'Yes or no?'

'Kill them!' screamed the Hadji Hassan. The Mullah appeared beside the Sheik. 'Kill them for the Glory of Allah!'

'Kill!' screamed the Arabs. 'Kill!'

'Answer,' yelled the Sheik. 'Answer or die!'

He paused, the shrieking Arabs paused with him and, before Corville could shout his defiance and touch off the fuse that would destroy the arsenal, the fort, and every living thing within it, the clear notes of a bugle echoed through the stillness.

'By God!' swore the legionnaire whom Corville had prevented from shooting the Sheik. 'They have arrived!' Even as he spoke he pressed the trigger and El Morini, a startled expression on his face, clutched at a red stain on his burnoose, staggered, and fell.

Immediately all hell broke loose.

Corville couldn't see the reinforcements but the attackers could and, as they stared at the long lines of marching legionnaires, they knew that their dreams of conquest were at an end. Desperate, half insane with hate, they turned their full fury on the tiny group remaining in the fortress. Guns splintered the walls with bullets, swords hacked at the bodies of dead and wounded and, like a screaming mass of animals, they hurled themselves against the final barricade.

Coldly Corville and the remaining legionnaires cut them down with machinegun fire. It wasn't battle. It was butchery and, as the reinforcements reached the fort, the attack broke and became a rout with tribes-men running from the long bayonets and spitting Lebels of the despised Ferengi.

'We're saved,' sobbed Clarice, for now that the danger was past, she broke down and became all-woman. 'We're saved!'

Corville held her close to him for a moment, then, as the blue and scarlet uniforms of the reinforcements mounted the walls and came towards him, gently pushed her into the arms of Miss Carson.

Colonel Le Farge grinned like a pleased tiger when he saw the body of El Morini.

'Who did this?'

'A legionnaire, I don't know his name.' Corville pointed out the man surrounded now by a bunch of cheering comrades. Le Farge called to him.

'Did you kill this man?'

'Yes, sir.'

'Good. You will receive promotion and extra wine.'

The legionnaire grinned, more at the promise of extra wine than promotion, and returned to his friends. Corville gestured to Le Farge.

'How did you get here so soon?'

'Thank your sergeant for that, I had men all ready to leave as soon as I learned where they would be needed most and, when Smith arrived more dead than alive, we set out on a forced march. Mon Dieu! How we marched! We have made history, I think. A third of our number fell out along the way and I, for one, can't blame them.'

'And Smith?'

'He came with us. He insisted and so I put him on a horse with two men to hold him on.' Le Farge stared over his shoulder. 'Here he is.'

Smith, his scarred face anxious, sighed as he saw the young officer. Automatically he gripped Corville's shoulders, then, seeming to remember himself, stiffened to attention and saluted.

'Your orders, sir?'

'Relax.' Corville smiled at the older man. 'We have much to talk over, you and I. One day, perhaps, I can thank you for all you have done, but now ... ' He gestured towards the huddled dead. 'Now we have work to do.'

'Yes, sir,' said the sergeant. 'I . . . '

He broke off as someone moved among the huddled shapes. It was the Mullah, Hadji Hassan and, as the tall man rose to his feet, he pointed a pistol at the young officer, 'Allah il Allah!' he shrieked. 'Dog of an unbeliever. Die!'

His finger closed around the trigger and flame spat directly towards Corville.

Smith moved. He threw himself forward just as the pistol fired and, as he smashed into the turbanned figure, blood streamed from his mouth as lead ripped into his body. Again the pistol fired, again, this time with a soggy sound, then the sergeant's bayonet had lanced into the Mullah's heart.

Smith was dying when they turned him over. He smiled up at Corville and, grasping the young man's hand, forced himself to speak.

'Tell your mother,' he whispered, then choked as blood filled his throat. 'Goodbye . . . son.'

'Goodbye father.' For a moment Corville stared down at the silent figure and, when he straightened, his eyes were moist with unshed tears.

'He was a hero,' said Le Farge sombrely. 'I had guessed, but it was not for me to say. And yet, even so, I am glad that you found him before it was too late.' His face hardened as he stared at the dead man. 'Marignay has much to answer for. We shall catch him and, instead of the clean, heroic death of a bullet, he will die like the dog he is. Unless, of course, the Arabs, now that we have broken their dreams of power, kill him first. I think I should like that. They will have no love for him and he is one man I could wish to die beneath their knives.' He sighed and rested his hand on the young man's shoulder.

'Your duty here is done. Leave your father to us who loved him. You have someone else to take care of now.'

He pushed the young man towards Clarice, standing beside the sobbing figure of Miss Carson, and as the young couple met, sighed again.

Corville would resign from the Legion now. He would take the news of his father's death back to his mother and, more than that, would take his intended wife too. Le Farge stared down at the dead and, as he stared, his arm lifted in salute.

'Adeiu, mes camarades,' he whispered. 'One day perhaps, we shall meet to fight again.'

Over the fort the proud tricolour of France floated in the freshening breeze and, even as they notes of the bugle died away, men were busy at their work among the dead.

It was the way of the Legion.

THE END

We do hope that you have enjoyed reading this large print book.

Did you know that all of our titles are available for purchase?

We publish a wide range of high quality large print books including:

Romances, Mysteries, Classics
General Fiction
Non Fiction and Westerns

Special interest titles available in large print are:

The Little Oxford Dictionary
Music Book, Song Book
Hymn Book, Service Book

Also available from us courtesy of Oxford University Press:

Young Readers' Dictionary
(large print edition)
Young Readers' Thesaurus
(large print edition)

For further information or a free brochure, please contact us at:
Ulverscroft Large Print Books Ltd.,
The Green, Bradgate Road, Anstey,
Leicester, LE7 7FU, England.
Tel: (00 44) **0116 236 4325**
Fax: (00 44) **0116 234 0205**

Other titles in the
Linford Mystery Library:

THE EMPTY COFFINS

John Russell Fearn

Two gruesome murders were discovered in the village of Little Payling. The bodies of a farmer and a local builder had been drained of blood. Their necks bore deep wounds, which centred on their jugular veins. When Scotland Yard arrived they made little progress — until Peter Malden became suspicious about his wife Elsie's first husband George Timperley, who had committed suicide. Then Elsie herself died and was buried — but her coffin, like George Timperley's, was found to be empty!